What was she doing? Zach Merrill didn't fit the profile of her ideal man.

It didn't matter that his eyes seemed to run right through her, that Olivia couldn't look at him without wondering what it would be like to touch him. He could never be hers. He was still in love with his wife and he was her employer and he had a daughter *and* she was living under his roof alongside his mother-in-law. Olivia forced herself to concentrate on his face.

"What else do you love?" Smiling blue eyes. "I'm curious."

She felt the breeze from the open window rippling over her bare arms, goose bumps prickling her skin. She didn't like talking about herself. With a camera around her neck, she knew who she was, but without it, when the lens was focused on her, her instinct was to hide. She rubbed at her lower lip with her thumb, tried to sound casual. "What do you want to know?"

Dear Reader,

Welcome to my second novel for Harlequin.

A year before I won the writing competition that launched my career as a romance writer, I photographed a friend's wedding in Italy. Later that same week, I traveled along the Amalfi Coast to visit the elegant town of Ravello. It was love at first sight! Walking through the streets of Ravello, glimpsing sea views through the open doorways of the hotels that lined the Via Santa Giovanni del Toro, I knew that one day I would write a love story set in this most romantic of locations.

As a former wedding photographer, I drew heavily on my own experience to create Zach and Olivia's emotional story. Widower Zach Merrill owns a prestige wedding venue located in the hills above Ravello. When his resident photographer is incapacitated after a moped accident, he asks Olivia Gardner to step in for the summer. For start-up wedding photographer Olivia, it's a dream job—as long as she can keep her head and hold on to her heart.

If you fall in love with Zach and Olivia, I'd love to hear from you on social media!

Ella x

Italian Summer with the Single Dad

Ella Hayes

HARLEQUIN

Romance

HARLEQUIN®

Romance™

Recycling programs
for this product may
not exist in your area.

ISBN-13: 978-1-335-55617-2

Italian Summer with the Single Dad

Copyright © 2020 by Ella Hayes

This edition published by arrangement with Harlequin Books S.A.

For questions and comments about the quality of this book,
please contact us at CustomerService@Harlequin.com.

Harlequin Enterprises ULC
22 Adelaide St. West, 40th Floor
Toronto, Ontario M5H 4E3, Canada
www.Harlequin.com

Printed in U.S.A.

After ten years as a television camerawoman, **Ella Hayes** started her own photography business so that she could work around the demands of her young family. As an award-winning wedding photographer, she's documented hundreds of love stories in beautiful locations, both at home and abroad. She lives in central Scotland with her husband and two grown-up sons. She loves reading, traveling with her camera, running and great coffee.

Books by Ella Hayes

Harlequin Romance

Her Brooding Scottish Heir

Visit the Author Profile page at Harlequin.com.

For Mum

**Praise for
Ella Hayes**

CHAPTER ONE

'TILT IT UP! No! More...more! There...no, there! Now, don't move.'

Olivia Gardner gripped the silver reflector and gritted her teeth. She couldn't understand why Ralph Holdsworth became so obnoxious the minute they arrived at a wedding. He was tolerable the rest of the time, albeit a little highly strung. He might be the go-to wedding photographer for those wealthy enough to afford him—his talent was undeniable—but assisting him was not the dream job she'd imagined. Most of the time she felt as if she was walking on eggshells. If she hadn't been learning so much about wedding photography she'd have walked out months ago.

He stepped back, lowered his camera and motioned to the bride. 'Okay, darling, let's move over to the window. Liv! The dress...?'

Olivia parked the reflector and dropped to her haunches, fanning out the dress the way

Ralph liked it. She hated the way he called all the brides 'darling'. How hard would it be to remember their names? She made a point of memorising the names of the entire bridal party ahead of any wedding.

Today's bride, Sophie, was a sweet-faced girl with porcelain skin, blonde hair and a slender figure. Her wedding dress was ivory silk embellished with tiny pearls and it felt soft and papery between Olivia's fingers as she pulled it out and smoothed it down. She tried to ignore Ralph's impatient glance as she moved onto the veil. It was a full veil, fine antique lace, a family heirloom probably. The bride's 'something old'.

Carefully, she draped the ornate edge over Sophie's shoulder and the girl smiled at her, mouthed a thank you. She could sense Sophie's nerves, gave her arm a little squeeze before she turned to pick up the reflector, but Ralph was waving an impatient hand in her direction.

'I don't need that now! Go pap some guests.'

She swallowed her irritation. She knew he didn't mean to be offhand, but it was annoying when he spoke to her like that in front of clients. Without a word, she picked up her camera and slipped out of the room.

Slowly she made her way along the wide hallway towards the staircase. She wished she had the courage to strike out on her own, but she was wary. She'd been down that road before. Armed with her photography degree, she'd started freelancing for an independent arts magazine but the circulation was low, the pay dismal. She'd stuck it out for a year to build a portfolio then tried to break into other magazines, but it was impossible. Magazines had their pet photographers.

She'd been working as a part-time barista when she met Ralph Holdsworth. He'd offered her a job and she'd jumped at it. He was a top wedding photographer, well-connected! At first he hadn't let her touch a camera. On wedding days she scurried around with reflectors, fluffed dresses and made sure that the right people were arranged into the right groups for the family photos. At the studio he set her to work editing an endless stream of wedding images which, he told her, would be an education in itself, and she handled all his paperwork too because he hated anything that wasn't creative. Twelve months and over forty weddings later, he'd given her a camera. She was to be his second shooter, responsible for the candid shots and the little details he didn't want to do, but he still expected her to help with the bridal portraits and to assemble the guests for the formal pictures.

Today's wedding was taking place in the garden of Kensall Manor, the bride's family home. The house was Tudor, all oak beams and half-panelled walls with mellow plaster above. On the galleried landing she paused to watch the comings and goings in the grand hall below: catering staff bustling about with trays, guests looking for somewhere to leave wedding gifts. And then the hall suddenly emptied. She was about to make a move when a tall, dark-haired man in a morning suit strode in carrying a shallow open box containing the men's buttonholes. There was something powerful in the set of his shoulders, something about him that made Olivia press herself closer to the balustrade to get a better view. He was looking around, for the groomsmen she supposed, then quite unexpectedly he looked up and caught her eye. She barely had time to catch her breath, to register the tiny, indefinable reaction in his eyes before he broke into a smile.

'Hello, up there! I don't suppose you've seen the bridegroom…?'

Blue eyes, something shining through them. She could feel her heart thumping in her chest, an unwelcome flush of heat rising through her as she called up a mental list of the wedding party. This had to be Zach Merrill, the groom's older brother and best man. As she cleared her throat to speak, she prayed that he wouldn't notice her blushing. 'No, I'm sorry, but if I see him I'll tell him the best man's looking for him.'

He looked bemused. 'How do you know I'm the—?'

'You're wearing the weight of responsibility on your shoulders...'

He lifted an eyebrow then broke into a smile which stole the breath from her lungs. 'Is it that obvious?'

She nodded.

'Zach!'

A man's voice rang out from somewhere off the hall and he turned to look, made a gesture of acknowledgement then lifted his eyes to hers once more.

'You can call off the search! I've found him.'

Blue eyes staring into hers. Somehow, she found her voice. 'That's lucky! Can't have a wedding without a groom.'

He laughed, started to walk away then stopped and looked up again. 'Goodbye then...'

She smiled softly. 'Bye.'

She watched him disappear then shook herself. Fraternising with the best man wasn't going to get her anywhere; she was supposed to be working. As she trotted down the stairs she pushed him to the back of her mind and tried to concentrate on the little tingle of excitement she always felt at the start of a wedding day.

She loved photographing weddings. Everything from the smallest details to the grandest gestures, but most of all she loved the ceremony. The way the bride and groom looked at each other...little nervous smiles, eyes glistening with happy tears. She found something compelling about the ritual of commitment, about the idea of two people starting out together, taking their first steps into uncharted waters. No loose ends. The thought of it always made her feel happy.

As she stepped out into the warm spring sunshine she hung the camera around her neck then followed the broad path that led to the southern aspect of the property. She could see guests mingling on the long terrace next to the house. She could hear the buzz of conversation and glasses tinkling and she knew she ought to go straight over, but instead she cut across the immaculate lawn to where rows of chevalier chairs were set out for a ceremony in front of the ornamental lake. It was perfect! She gazed at the scene, lifted her camera and put her eye to the viewfinder. For a moment she pictured herself in the frame, standing with the man she loved, her fingers laced in his, their eyes locked, lips pledging love and fidelity, and then…the kiss.

She lowered the camera and watched a lone coot swimming across the glassy surface of the lake. She wished she could switch off her old teenage fantasy but it was always there in her head, playing on a loop. She didn't understand where her silly romantic notions came from. Her own parents had never married—they were far too modern for that!

She came back to herself and glanced over her shoulder. If Ralph caught her staring down the aisle when there were guests to photograph she'd soon be out of a job. It didn't take much to set him off when he was in the thick of a wedding shoot. She supposed he was a victim of his own success—under pressure to produce astonishing images all the time. The last thing she wanted to do was provoke him. Besides, she thought as she made her way towards the terrace, 'papping' guests was a step up from carrying his camera bag, even if she knew that she was capable of so much more.

From the periphery she scanned the crowd then lifted the camera with its long paparazzi lens. She snapped close-ups of smiling faces, bright hats, animated groups. She moved around, working the different angles, picking out details—champagne flutes sparkling on a tray, an elegant woman with immaculate red lipstick and long red nails. She spied a little girl with dark serious eyes peering through a sea of legs. She was a pretty little thing, so Olivia crouched down to play peek-a-boo from behind the camera. The girl buried her small fingers into the fabric of a woman's skirt, eyes brightening. Olivia pulled a funny face and the girl returned a shy smile. She fired a burst of frames then winked at the child and stood up. She liked photographing children—no hang-ups, no vanity.

With a couple of hundred shots done, she left the terrace and walked across the lawn to take some wider views. The old house must have been extended over the years. She could see the different materials in the two wings that flanked the original Tudor construction but the meld was pleasing, the exterior softened with an ancient wisteria and a rampant, scrambling clematis. All Ralph's clients owned properties like this. Sometimes she couldn't believe that this was her life now: every weekend spent in some elegant home or some fancy hotel. It was a far cry from the small Sussex cottage where she'd grown up.

She checked her watch. The great hall would be set for the wedding breakfast by now, which meant she'd be able to photograph the room in its pristine state. Lifting the camera from around her neck, she set off towards the front of the house but as she stepped onto the sweeping driveway she stopped, toes pressed to the tarmac. Up ahead, the groom was chatting and laughing with his two groomsmen—and Zach! She felt her heart flip over and land in her stomach. The way Zach was standing, the way his shoulders shifted under his morning coat as he moved… It would be so easy just to stand and watch…

Get a grip.

She took a deep breath and forced her feet to move. There was no avoiding an encounter if she wanted to get back into the house, so she'd just have to play it cool. As she drew nearer, she tried to concentrate on the ushers' names. Charlie and Will—or was it Bill? Cousins anyway. They were a little shorter than the Merrill brothers and infinitely less nervous from the look of things.

Far too soon she found herself standing in front of the little group.

'Good morning!' She could feel Zach looking at her, but she fixed her eyes on the groom. 'Lucas, we haven't met before. I'm Olivia Gardner, Ralph Holdsworth's assistant.'

Lucas extended a hand and shook hers

warmly. 'Hi, Olivia. Pleased to meet you.' She noticed a tiny fleck of toothpaste at the corner of his mouth, the lopsided rose on his lapel. He motioned to Zach. 'This is my brother, Zach, and these good-for-nothing hangers-on are Charlie and Will.'

Charlie threw a playful punch at Lucas's arm. 'Good-for-nothing hangers-on? You're going to pay for that!'

As a friendly skirmish broke out, Zach stepped into the space between herself and the jostling men. It was a gallant protective gesture but it meant that he was now rather close. She took a little step back, lifted her eyes hesitantly.

He rolled his eyes then smiled. 'See what I have to put up with?' He held out his hand. 'It's nice to meet you properly, Olivia. Are you here all day?'

His palm was warm and dry. It felt nice. 'Yes. Until after the first dance…'

'It's a long day for you.' His gaze shifted to the camera in her hand. 'That looks heavy.'

His dark hair was on the long side, combed back from a lightly tanned face. She noticed fine lines etched into the skin around his eyes and, now that she was close, she could see kindness in his gaze, something else too that

she couldn't quite pin down. She suddenly realised it was her turn to speak.

'It is… Heavy, I mean…but you get used
to it.'

Lucas was straightening his jacket. 'Will
you take a picture of us, Olivia?'

'Of course.' She hung the camera around
her neck and stepped forward. 'Can I sort your
buttonhole first?'

He glanced at the crooked rose on his lapel
and pulled a face. 'Charlie, you idiot! You've
roughed me up.'

She smiled. 'It wasn't Charlie's fault.' She
flipped over Lucas's lapel, pulled out the
long pin then fixed it back into place. 'Roses
are heavy—they can easily slip to the side if
they're not pinned properly.'

'Is mine okay?'

Zach was looking at her. She tried to ignore
the little rush of heat rising through her as she
stepped towards him and turned back the lapel
of his jacket. This close, she could smell his
cologne—citrus top note, woody base.

He lifted his chin while she worked at the
pin. 'You have an eye for detail.'

'It's an occupational necessity.' She lowered
her voice as she re-pinned the flower. 'Lucas
has toothpaste at the corner of his mouth. Perhaps you could mention it to him before I take

the photo…?' She stepped back and lifted her eyes to his. 'Okay?'

There was amusement on his face as he adjusted his collar. 'No problem.'

She turned away and drew a steadying breath. Zach Merrill was giving her vertigo. As she put some distance between herself and the group, she felt her heart drumming against her chest and when she turned around to line up the photograph and adjust the camera settings she was all fingers and thumbs. She took another deep breath. 'Okay, gentlemen—' Four pairs of eyes looked her way. 'Lucas and Zach, can you stand shoulder to shoulder, please, then Charlie and Will, can you take the wings?'

'Wingmen!' Will laughed. 'I like that!'

They shuffled into position and Olivia framed the shot. It was hard to concentrate on Lucas when Zach's face kept drawing her eye, but she simply had to—it was *Lucas's* day— she had to make sure that *he* looked perfect. She took some shots, adjusted the zoom, took a few more and then suddenly she went cold. Ralph always photographed the groom and his attendants. She wasn't supposed to be doing this.

'Can we do a fun one?' Lucas was looking at her expectantly.

She smiled. 'What did you have in mind?'

Her stomach was churning. She couldn't refuse. Lucas *was* the client after all, but Ralph was going to arrive at any moment and he wouldn't like it.

Zach was smiling at her and there was something in his eyes that chased her fears away. 'He wants to do a leaning shot. Look! We'll show you.'

She glanced at the big entrance door. No sign of Ralph—hopefully, he was still busy with Sophie and the bridesmaids. She tried to push him out of her thoughts as she watched Lucas and the men arranging themselves into a line. On a count of three, they canted their bodies at a forty-five-degree angle and burst out laughing. She couldn't help laughing too and fired off a succession of frames. This was what she loved about photographing weddings, being part of spontaneous moments like this.

'Olivia!'

The camera skewed in her hands. She took a breath and looked over to the vast doorway where Ralph was standing, rigid as a statue. A small shiver of guilt forked through her limbs and then slowly, deliberately, she tucked it away. She'd done nothing wrong. He was just being cranky as usual. She looked over at the men, who were still laughing and jostling each other. They didn't seem to have noticed anything and she was relieved. She pinned on a bright smile and stepped towards them.

'Ralph's here to take your formal pictures now.' She could feel Zach's eyes on her but forced herself to look at Lucas. 'Have fun! I'll see you later.'

As she walked towards the house she wondered if Zach was still watching her, but then she pushed the thought away because Ralph was waiting for her in the doorway, his eyes flinty, his mouth a grim straight line.

Zach Merrill couldn't help noticing the way Olivia had reacted to Holdsworth's voice. She'd sort of curled into herself, then quickly conjured up some fake brightness before walking away. He'd watched the pair of them talking in the doorway. He couldn't read their lips but he could read their body language. For some reason Holdsworth had been remonstrating with her, and from the tilt of her chin he could tell she'd been fighting her corner, whatever that might be.

He couldn't imagine what Holdsworth was upset about. Olivia Gardner struck him as polite and professional. How subtly she'd handled the issue with the lopsided rose on his brother's lapel, the rogue spot of toothpaste. She had an eye for detail, an easy, engaging manner, a lovely smile… She was clearly an asset and he hoped that Holdsworth could see it. Zach certainly knew which one of them he preferred. He came back to the moment, focused on what Holdsworth was saying.

'Okay, guys, walk forward now, swing your arms, talk to each other…laughing's good, keep it natural.'

The photographer was lying on his stomach, a plastic sheet spread out beneath him. He was pointing a camera in their direction. They only had to walk towards him but he was making them do it again and again; it was getting hard to keep up the fake chatter and laughter. As they set off for the umpteenth time Lucas leaned in and whispered to him that Holdsworth was costing Sophie's parents a small fortune so maybe doing every shot a hundred times was how he justified his fee. They both laughed out loud at that one, then laughed all over again when Holdsworth called out, 'That's the money shot!'

He was doing his best to be sociable, but now that the ceremony was over Zach was feeling restless. He'd caught up with his family, mingled with the guests, but he'd only been half listening to conversations, smiling in all the right places. It was his brother's wedding: a special occasion. He knew he ought to be enjoying himself, but it felt too much like work. He'd rather have been talking to the band. He'd seen them rocking up in their van, jaunty strides as they unloaded their amps and speakers, the big black cases for drums and keyboards. Guitars!

He lifted a fresh glass from a passing tray and retreated to a quiet corner of the terrace. He watched Holdsworth directing Lucas and Sophie into romantic poses at the lakeside, waving his hands about, cameras swinging from his shoulders, full of nervous energy. An image flashed into his head—Olivia and Holdsworth in the doorway—an altercation. He scanned the edges of the crowd, looking for the girl's nimble figure, her chestnut ponytail, the red camera strap around her neck, but she was nowhere to be seen.

She'd been there during the formal family photos, organising them all. Addressing them by name, adjusting ties and corsages, gentle hands on shoulders—turn this way a little please—flashing her warm, bright smile. He hadn't been able to take his eyes off her. She was lovely...and so good with people, so polished. She'd caught his eye a couple of times and then she'd smiled and blushed a little bit and he'd found himself smiling too because she was flirting with him and for some reason he liked it. In no time at all the family photo session was done. It had gone so smoothly that if he hadn't seen them fighting he would have assumed that Olivia and Holdsworth were the best of friends.

He shifted his gaze back to the lake. Lucas was facing Sophie now, forehead to forehead. Sophie was giggling and Holdsworth was calling out instructions from behind the camera. 'Keep it! Hold it!'

He felt a smile growing on his lips. Sophie and Lucas were besotted with each other, perfect for one another. He could see a happy future for them because they were soulmates. That was what he'd written in his speech anyway, but as a deep ache filled his heart he wondered if he'd be able to say those words at all. The climbing voices around him suddenly felt too loud. He parked his glass and slipped away into the garden.

The grounds of Kensall Manor were extensive. As he walked, the voices on the terrace dwindled to a burble then gave way to birdsong. He passed through a wrought iron gate into an orchard and wandered through gnarled apple trees laden with blossom, alive with the buzzing and humming of bees. He let his mind drift to memories of his own wedding day. He could still see Izzy walking towards him through the lemon trees, patches of sunlight dappling on her skin, splashing the silk chiffon of her dress. She'd had that look in her eye, that secret smile she kept for him alone. His heart had buckled in his chest as she'd turned towards him and threaded her fingers into his. She had been his one perfect love, his life, his everything, and now she was gone, snatched from him in a tragic instant. He swallowed hard, plucked a blossom from a low branch. Marrying your soulmate was not a passport to a happy future. The future was as delicate and destructible as the flower he held in his hand.

He drew a steadying breath and checked his watch. He wondered if Alessia had woken from her nap yet. So many new faces, and this big strange house in the English countryside— it was bound to be tiring for a three-year-old. He hadn't been sure about bringing her at all, but of course his mother was always keen to see her granddaughter, and Lucas had insisted that his little niece should come to the wedding.

He crushed the flower between his fingers and let it fall to the ground. In half an hour the guests were going to be seated for the wedding breakfast and the more he thought about his speech, the more anxious he felt. He checked his inside pocket, touched the paper folded up inside. He wasn't nervous about speaking in public—as a hotelier, talking to people was an integral part of his life—but the speech he'd written about soulmates and everlasting love would unravel him, he just knew it. Perhaps if he altered some lines here and there, skimmed over the emotional stuff, he'd manage to hold it together. He just needed a pen and a quiet place to do it.

'Oh, I'm sorry—' He stopped mid-stride, the breath catching in his throat. Olivia Gardner was sitting in front of a laptop surrounded by camera equipment. 'I was told this room was empty.'

'It's almost empty.' She smiled hesitantly. 'There's only me here.'

He noticed a faint colour in her cheeks as she held his gaze. He noticed his own pulse. 'Can I come in?'

'Of course.'

He stepped into the room and closed the door. 'I need to look at my speech.'

She plugged a device into the side of her laptop. 'Don't mind me—if you want to practise, I mean.'

'It's not speaking I'm worried about.' He

reached into his pocket for the thin wad of paper. 'I need to revise what I'm saying.'

'Ah.' She pressed a key and looked up. 'I get it! You're having second thoughts about giving your brother a roasting…?'

'Something like that.' He couldn't tell her that he was trying to avoid embarrassing himself. 'I don't suppose you've got a pen?'

'I have.' She rooted through the pockets of the jacket hanging over the back of her chair. 'Somewhere…'

He stepped closer, noticed thumbnail images filling the computer screen.

'Here!' She was holding out a silver pen, warm brown eyes fixed on his.

'Thanks.' He took the pen, motioned to the laptop. 'Editing already?'

'No. Just downloading and backing up. We bank images as we go along, just in case.'

'Can I see some?'

She glanced at the door and it wasn't hard to read her thoughts.

'You don't have to worry—Holdsworth's at the lake with Lucas and Sophie.' He smiled. 'It can be our little secret.'

She hesitated then met his gaze squarely. 'It's not—Ralph's a very talented photographer—'

'Who's difficult to work with, I imagine…?'

Her lips were quirking into a half-smile. 'He can be challenging…'

'Extremely challenging, from what I've seen.'

She was pressing her lips together hard, trying to suppress a smile but her eyes were giving her away. 'Ralph's…okay.'

She might have issues with her boss but she was keeping them to herself. Zach admired her loyalty though he wondered if Holdsworth deserved it.

'I'd really like to see your pictures. What about the photo you took of us leaning? Will you show me that one at least?'

She scrunched her face up. 'Well, I do have to flag some photos for a slideshow… I suppose if you *happened* to be sitting close by, you might *accidentally* see some images…'

The mischievous gleam in her eye was irresistible. He knew he ought to be looking at his speech, but his curiosity about her was getting the better of him. She struck him as talented and he wanted to know if he was right. He sat beside her then opened up his speech and smoothed it out on the table. There was something joyful about the little conspiracy they were sharing and when he spoke he couldn't keep the smile out of his voice. 'I'll just work on my speech…'

She turned to face him, eyebrows arching. 'And I'll go through the pictures I took this morning...'

For a long moment he held her gaze. He noticed the curve of her cheek, the wisp of hair falling against her neck, the sweet shape of her mouth and he noticed the way her expression was changing, how the light in her eyes felt like a soft pocket of warmth—felt like home. Confused suddenly, he forced himself to look away and concentrate on the screen.

Her pictures were good! Sharp, clear, well-composed. The leaning shot made him laugh—Lucas was going to love it. She'd caught some great candid moments on the terrace too. When he saw a familiar little face with thick dark lashes the breath caught in his throat.

'Stop!'

'You want to see this one?'

He nodded.

With a click, she enlarged the image so that his daughter's face filled the screen. He stared at the photograph. Alessia was wearing her mother's secret smile. She was a happy little girl but he'd never seen that smile on her face before. Suddenly he felt disorientated, stranded between the past and the present.

Olivia leaned back in her chair. 'She's lovely, isn't she? Is she a relative?'

'Yes.' He swallowed hard. 'Alessia is my daughter.'

'Oh!' She looked shocked then a little embarrassed. 'I didn't know she was yours…'

Two spots of colour were blooming on her cheeks and instantly he felt guilty. She hadn't seen him with Alessia. His mother had been babysitting all day, and Alessia had been taking a nap while the family photos were being taken. Olivia knew nothing about his situation. All she knew was that he'd been catching her eye all day, smiling at her, receptive to her flirting. Maybe he'd even encouraged it. He'd have to think about that later, but right now he owed her an explanation.

'Her name is Alessia.' He swallowed. 'The way you've caught her—her smile. She looks just like her mother.'

He noticed Olivia glancing at the gold band on his left hand, noticed a new flush of colour creeping upwards from the base of her throat.

'Is your wife—?'

'No! She isn't here.' With difficulty, he held her gaze. 'She passed away two years ago.'

Olivia's face crumpled. 'Oh, no. No! I'm so sorry.' Her words escaped in a gasp and she lifted her hand as if she was going to touch him, but she didn't, just held his gaze with glistening eyes. 'Alessia must have been a baby.'

He nodded slowly. 'We'd just celebrated her first birthday...' In his mind he could see Izzy holding the lemon birthday cake she'd made, icing sugar in her hair and on her nose, and that scary moment when Alessia had reached out to touch the single burning candle. He'd blown it out just in time.

Olivia turned to look at the screen. 'If Alessia looks like her mother, your wife must have been beautiful.'

'She was...' He watched her, staring at the screen, chewing her lip. He supposed she was taking it all in, feeling foolish perhaps... He couldn't tell her he was feeling foolish too. He'd never expected to feel attracted to his brother's wedding photographer, never expected to be sitting beside her, breathing in the scent of her perfume, telling her about his wife and daughter.

The mounting noise of footsteps and voices in the hall outside seemed to draw a line under the moment and it was a relief. He ran a hand through his hair. 'I'd better go... Everyone's coming in...' He folded up his untouched speech. 'Looks like I'm going with the speech as it is.'

'I'm sure it'll be great!' She smiled. 'Actually, it better be great because I'll be taking pictures during the speeches—you need to give me some good moments!'

There was something reassuring in her gaze, something that bolstered his spirits. He got to his feet, slipped the pen into his pocket. 'I'll do my best.'

Olivia adjusted her ponytail and fanned her face with her hands. The great hall was warm in the aftermath of dinner, but it wasn't the only reason her cheeks felt hot. She was still reeling from everything Zach had told her, felt so stupid for thinking...for imagining... *How* had she managed not to notice his wedding ring? So much for supposedly having an eye for detail!

She looked across to the top table. He was scribbling furiously on a piece of paper—revising his speech after all. His mother was sitting in the next seat with Alessia on her knee. Alessia was clasping a crayon, bent over a colouring book, concentrating hard, except for the moments when she stopped to look at Zach. Alessia was copying him and he had no idea. Fathers and daughters... She pushed the thought away, lifted the camera and snapped a lady in a pink hat blowing bubbles from a tiny bottle.

Zach had let her down gently she supposed,

but the more she thought about it, the more she realised that he'd been at it too with his lingering looks and little smiles during the family photos—it definitely wasn't her imagination.

She scanned the room for more photo opportunities, snapped a man putting on his wife's hat, acting the fool. She looked at Zach again. His lips were moving, rehearsing the new words he'd written, her silver pen glinting in his hand.

Maybe the truth was that they were attracted to each other, but a random wedding day crush wasn't going to lead to anything, especially since a widower with a daughter was the last thing she was looking for.

Too complicated!

She didn't like loose ends. She liked things cut and dried, wanted someone she could build a life with, not someone who had a life she'd have to fit into. She glanced at Alessia. She knew nothing about small children, didn't see herself as a stepmother. She was only twenty-four; she was still carving out a career. Emotional entanglements would only take her eye off the ball. She had to push forward, seize opportunities…

She scanned the room, saw Ralph talking to a young couple then discreetly handing them a business card. Networking was easy for him—

he had a good reputation, a solid client base. If she started up on her own she'd have to break in and that was difficult, especially since she wanted high-end clients.

Yet again she found her gaze drifting back to the top table. *Zach* had really liked her photographs. He might recommend her to people he knew. The Merrill family owned a hotel chain after all… Suddenly he looked up, straight into her eyes and there it was again, that feeling that there was something between them. She smiled back quickly and looked away. No! She wouldn't be able to ask Zach for any favours. He only had to look at her and her head started to spin.

When she saw the Master of Ceremonies approaching the top table to announce the speeches, she lifted her camera. Photographing the speeches was another concession Ralph had made to her. She needed to focus on getting great pictures because, until she found the courage to break out on her own, she needed this job.

CHAPTER TWO

Six weeks later...

OLIVIA MADE HER way down the aisle of the bus and sank into a seat. She hefted her camera bag onto the vacant seat beside her and rummaged in her other bag for her sunglasses. In spite of the tinted windows, it seemed too bright. Bright and sunny and warm. Deliciously warm!

As she watched the other passengers piling aboard with belongings of all shapes and sizes, she had the urge to pinch herself yet again, just in case she was dreaming. Was she really here in Italy, on the final leg of her journey to start a new job in Ravello?

The bus belched, lurched then pulled away from the airport bus stop, cruising slowly to the exit before joining a busy road. The sun glinted off the chrome of unfamiliar cars, dappled through the leaves of unfamiliar trees and she felt her lips curving into a smile. It *was* real, and it was all because of what had happened after the Merrill wedding...

They'd been driving back to London when Ralph had suddenly announced that he was letting her go.

She couldn't believe her ears. 'You're letting me go! Why? Because I took a few photographs of the groomsmen? For goodness' sake, Ralph.'

'It's not that.'

'What then?'

He threw her a sheepish look. 'Because you're after my job!'

'I'm not!'

He pulled up at a set of traffic lights and turned to face her. 'Okay, I'm not saying you want *my* exact job, but you want more than I can give you. I'm not looking for a partner, Liv. I want an assistant. At the very most I want someone who's happy shooting the flowers and the frilly bits—a few guests now and again. You, my darling, want to be *the* photographer with a capital F.'

'It's P! And yes, I won't deny that I want to be a wedding photographer...one day...but I'm not ready.'

'You're more than ready.' The traffic light changed and Ralph drove on. 'I watched you working with those boys today and you were great. You get on with people, your technical skills are top-notch. It's time for you to fly the nest.'

She felt as if the air was rearranging itself around her. Ralph had been getting on her nerves for ever, but this wasn't what she'd planned—she didn't have a plan. Maybe that was the problem. She'd spent most of her time with Ralph just simmering with frustration, but she'd never done anything about it. She hadn't imagined that he would be the one to push her off the plank.

'Don't look so glum, darling. You can have some of my old gear as a leaving present.' He tipped her a wink. 'You're going to be a big success. Just make sure you're not a big success on my patch!'

After the initial shock, she realised that he was right. Letting her go was a backhanded compliment. Although the thought of launching herself as a wedding photographer was scary, she knew she had the skills, and handling Ralph's admin had given her a good insight into the business side of things. Her biggest challenge was going to be finding the right clients, but then...

On her very last afternoon Ralph muttered something about having left some kit for her as promised, then he'd shot off to some 'important' meeting which didn't seem to be marked in the diary. When she went into his office and saw what he'd put out for her she was overwhelmed. Some of the gear had hardly been used, just mothballed in favour of something newer or fancier. She was looking at everything he'd given her, feeling a bit emotional about it, when the telephone had rung.

'Good afternoon. Holdsworth Photography.'

'Hello. Is that Olivia Gardner?'

The man's voice was familiar. Probably one of Ralph's bridegrooms. 'Yes. Can I help—?'

'I have something of yours…' Little pause. 'It's got your name engraved on it.'

'Something of mine?' A rapid clicking sound filled her ears and suddenly she knew why she'd recognised his voice. 'Zach Merrill! You've got my pen!'

'I forgot to give it back… I'm so sorry.'

She could hear the smile in his voice, momentarily lost herself in a memory of intent blue eyes. 'There's no need to apologise. You were stressing about your speech, if I remember rightly. In such circumstances, petty theft is excusable.' She couldn't stop smiling, couldn't help feeling a little glow at the thought of him, even if he was absolutely not her dream man.

'It was very good, by the way—your speech, and I've heard lots of speeches—'

'Thanks! I'm not so sure, but I'll take your word for it.'

His voice in her ear sounded warm, intimate somehow. She was blushing, glad that he couldn't see her face. She cleared her throat, tried to sound blasé. 'So—about the pen. It was a twenty-first birthday present—can I have it back?'

'Of course. You might even want to collect it in person…'

His voice was playful. She felt her forehead creasing, a smile lifting the corners of her mouth. 'Okay, you've got my attention.'

'Actually, this isn't just about the pen—' His tone downshifted, became serious. 'I need to talk to you about something. Calling you at work was the only way I could reach you, but it's not a conversation we can have if Holdsworth's about.'

'He's not here—but it wouldn't matter anyway. It's my last day today.'

'Your last day! You've got a new job?' He sounded disappointed.

She chewed her bottom lip. She was growing more confused by the second. 'No.' Deep breath. 'Actually, I'm going out on my own.'

'Ahh.' He was smiling again, she could tell.

'Well, in that case I'll get straight to the point. You may remember that my family owns a chain of hotels.'

She could feel her heart thumping. 'Yes.'

'In addition, I own an exclusive wedding venue. High-end. We look after everything: accommodation, catering, ceremony and…photography.' His voice tightened. 'I've just come off the phone with my photographer, Michele. Some idiot knocked him off his moped, fractured his leg. Poor guy's going to be out of action for at least six weeks.' He sighed. 'So, here's the thing… I'm booked solid and I need a wedding photographer to fill in—someone I can trust.'

Olivia's head began to spin so fast that it took a moment for everything to sink in. Was Zach Merrill offering her a succession of high-end wedding clients on a plate? She felt her spine tingle. This was her moment, her chance to prove herself. She tried to calm her galloping heart with a slow, measured breath. 'You're asking *me* to step into your photographer's shoes?'

'Yes. I've seen the quality of your work, the way you interact with people. You'd be perfect, I know you would. Is there any way you could help me out?'

Ah—let me see...

'Yes! That is, I want to say yes, but I have so many questions! I mean—I don't even know where your venue is—although I've worked in a lot of places with Ralph so I might know it.'

He'd laughed then. 'I doubt it. Casa Isabella is in Ravello.'

'As in—Italy?'

'That's right.'

'Wow!'

After his call, she'd looked at Casa Isabella online, scrolled through the website pages with wide, excited eyes. It was a grand old *palazzo*, slightly faded but elegant. Its secluded hillside setting above Ravello offered spectacular views of the Tyrrhenian Sea from its terrace and balconies, but it was the garden that had taken her breath away. Ancient cypress trees on terraced lawns, a stone pond with a sparkling fountain, arches leading to secret garden rooms with weathered statues. Achingly romantic, it was a wedding photographer's dream venue…

And now she was here, all set to photograph six weddings in a prestige venue—in Italy! Portfolio couples! She felt sick with nerves, a little dizzy, high on adrenaline, still incredulous but happy and excited too. No wonder she kept wanting to pinch herself.

She pulled a bottle of water from her bag

and took a steadying sip as the poor dwellings on the outskirts of Naples gave way to hillsides covered in olive trees. The bus trundled through small towns with narrow streets, screeched to a halt more than once to avoid scooters weaving through the traffic. She gazed at the sun-baked terracotta roofs, so different to roofs in England. She got her phone out, took pictures through the window—ancient churches, walls covered in brightly scrambling bougainvillea. She watched people going about their day-to-day business, saw people sitting at roadside cafés reading the papers or chatting with friends. Between the towns, she glimpsed lemon groves behind crumbling walls and then, on the skyline, she saw the mighty Vesuvius, its peak rising into a smear of hazy cloud.

She sipped her water again and thought about Zach. Now that he was going to be her boss, it was inappropriate to think about him in anything other than a platonic way, yet when she pictured his eyes, recalled how handsome he'd looked at Lucas and Sophie's wedding, she felt a little glow of anticipation that made her lips curve upwards into a secret little smile.

Zach Merrill leaned against the wing of his convertible, pushed his sunglasses onto his head and looked along the valley, searching the twisting road for signs of Olivia's bus. He couldn't believe how things had worked out. After Michele had called him from the hospital, he'd contacted some photographers he knew, but none of them were free. Calling Olivia had been a long shot, but he'd seen that she was tired of working for Holdsworth, had hoped that she would consider his offer. How lucky that she'd been free to come.

His fingers closed around the pen in his pocket. He remembered the look in her eyes when she'd handed it to him, warm light pouring into him, making him dizzy. He'd had to look away, force himself to concentrate on the pictures filling her computer screen, but it was lucky too that he'd seen those photographs, seen the quality of her work. If he hadn't—Alessia's face captured so perfectly—he might not have thought of her as a replacement for Michele at all.

He pulled the pen from his pocket, ran his finger over the inscription. He hadn't meant to steal her twenty-first birthday pen. He hadn't been himself that day...noticing Olivia with her bright brown hair and warm smile, liking the way she was looking at him, the way she was flirting, and then he'd been remembering Izzy and worrying about his speech. Emotions piling up, layers of confusion, his feelings all over the place…and then seeing Alessia's face in the photograph…so like her mother's.

And now Olivia was on her way to Ravello, as if some invisible ink was drawing them together.

He slipped the pen back into his pocket. His mother-in-law, Lucia, had questioned why he was bringing an untested photographer all the way from England—*'Couldn't you get someone from Naples?'*

He'd told her that the decent people were already booked for the summer. He'd pointed out that Olivia was a native English speaker, which was perfect because their clients were mostly English-speaking. Besides, he'd added, wasn't it the decent thing to do, to give a talented person a break? She'd agreed but she'd had a knowing look in her eye which bothered him. Maybe she thought that having Olivia to stay at Casa Isabella was going to change things. He could understand that in a way.

Turning the faded *palazzo* into an exclusive wedding venue had been Izzy's idea—their dream project. They'd started on the interior renovations and then Izzy had found the original landscape plans in the attic. After that, she'd worked closely with the gardeners to restore the old pathways and formal beds, breathing life back into the neglected garden. She'd get so excited about the smallest thing: new shoots on old wood, some jaded creeper bursting into flower... He'd loved Izzy with all his heart. He missed her every day. But he didn't appreciate his mother-in-law dissecting his motives for bringing Olivia here. It was a business decision. He needed a wedding photographer and Olivia was talented, professional and discreet. Plus, she was available. That was all there was to it.

When the bus finally came into view he rocked forward off the car and lowered his sunglasses, trying to ignore the little knot of excitement tightening in his stomach. After she'd agreed to come he'd phoned her a few times to discuss practical matters like getting her a computer. He'd enjoyed their conversations. He'd liked her enthusiasm, but talking to her, hearing the vitality in her voice, had made him realise how jaded he felt. He was married to the business, worked like a dog, but he didn't feel fulfilled. He felt restless.

When the bus pulled in and Olivia bumped down the steps with her camera bag he almost didn't recognise her—she looked so different to the way she'd looked at the wedding. She was wearing blue sneakers, faded jeans and a white top which was slipping off her shoulder. Her hair was twisted into a loose knot and most of her face was hidden by a very large pair of sunglasses. The sight of her made him ridiculously happy. He had to fight the urge to pick her up and swing her around. Instead he held out his hand. 'Olivia! Welcome to Ravello.'

She pushed her sunglasses up and stretched her hand to his. 'Zach! It's so nice to see you, and please—call me Liv. Everyone else does!'

'Okay, Liv.' He smiled. The sunlight catching her eyes made them look lighter than he remembered, like amber, and for the first time he noticed the darker ring around the edge of her irises. When he realised he was still holding her hand he let it go quickly and reached for her camera bag. 'How was your journey?'

'It was great, although I can see how Michele got hurt. The roads here are challenging, and as for the way people drive—'

The bus driver set down a modest suitcase and another big camera bag. Zach handed him a tip then picked up her other bags. 'You see a lot of dented cars around here, that's for sure! Is this the only luggage you've got?'

'I travel light.' She widened her eyes. 'Except for the camera gear!'

'I suppose it's just as well…' He motioned to his car.

'Nice!' She walked over, ran her fingers over the silver paintwork. 'It's not even dented!'

She was teasing him, laughing, and he couldn't help laughing too. 'I don't get out much.' He put her bags in the back and opened the door for her. 'Ready?'

'Absolutely!' She slipped her sunglasses over her eyes and beamed.

She felt the sun warming her face as Zach drove them up into the hills. It felt so good to see him again. As the bus had pulled in, the sight of him waiting for her had set her heart going—she'd been glad of her dark glasses. He'd looked handsome at the wedding, but today, casually dressed in a pale blue shirt and navy chinos, he looked even better. More relaxed. From behind her sunglasses she took in the golden skin at the base of his throat, the nice shape of his mouth, the straight nose. His dark hair had been combed back at the wedding, but now it was blowing every which way in the breeze, dishevelled, touchable.

He glanced at her and smiled. 'What do you think so far?'

Gorgeous.

She blushed, wondered if he'd noticed her checking him out. She turned to look at the view. 'It's lovely, greener than I imagined and so warm.'

'I'm sorry I couldn't pick you up in Naples. I had a meeting sprung on me at the last minute.'

'That's okay—the bus ride was an education.'

His shirt sleeves were rolled back. It was hard not to notice his forearms. Tanned, muscular. She forced herself to concentrate on the view: slopes thick with sturdy shrubs and olive trees, a pair of donkeys in a paddock, tails flicking. She adjusted her sunglasses, glanced at him again. How old was he? Early thirties perhaps—at least six years older than she was—and married.

Widowed.

She wondered about his wife. He'd had so much to cope with: grief, a young baby and a business too. *'I don't get out much.'* Did he ever get lonely?

On a tight bend thick with trees he steered the car into a concealed entrance and stopped in front of tall iron gates set into a stone wall. Engraved on a simple plaque fixed to the wall were the words *Casa Isabella*.

He pushed his sunglasses up, turned to face her. 'Isabella was my wife's name—Izzy.' She noticed the way he drew in a breath. 'When we get to the house you'll meet my mother-in-law, Lucia. She helps me with Alessia.'

Olivia sensed that she didn't need to reply.

'Lucia's a strong woman, an incredible person, and I couldn't have coped without her these past two years.' A shadow crossed his face. 'She's grateful to you for coming at such short notice but...she's a little unsettled... maybe because this was Izzy's home.' He turned to press a button on the dash and the gates started to move. 'I wanted to tell you, just in case you pick up a vibe...' He met her eye again and suddenly he smiled. 'I'm probably worrying too much. You're really good with people—it won't be a problem.'

As he slid the car through the gates she tried not to think about Lucia, the admirable but possibly hostile mother-in-law. Instead, she looked back at the gates closing behind them. 'Do you need such tight security here?'

'Not really, but we had a celebrity wedding last year—they insisted on gates.'

She wanted to know more, but she didn't want to seem star-struck so she nodded and tried to look blasé as he drove them through a terraced vineyard and onwards through an ancient olive grove. Under the shade of the olive trees the light was blue-green, thick as gauze.

She made a mental note to go back with her camera some time, try to capture it.

Emerging into the sunshine, the road continued through an area of rough pasture, then turned sharply to the right. As Casa Isabella came into view, framed by an avenue of tall cypress trees, she gasped softly. Whitewashed in pale ochre, roofed with weathered pantiles, the ground floor windows were tall and shuttered, arranged at identical intervals along the length of the house. In the centre, an imposing double stairway led to a vast oak door. She knew from the website that on the other side of the property, facing the sea, was a long, arched veranda opening out to the wide terrace where the wedding ceremonies took place. Beyond the terrace, over the stone balcony, and all around the property lay the enchanting garden.

'Papà! Papà!'

Olivia watched Alessia run into Zach's arms, watched him swing her up, cuddle her in. He rattled off something in Italian then lowered his voice, adopted a coaxing tone until Alessia turned dark eyes towards her. He cautioned gently. 'In English, remember...'

Alessia licked her lips. 'Hello, Olivia. Welcome to Casa Isabella.' She smiled quickly then buried her face into Zach's shirt, giggling.

Olivia stepped forward hesitantly. Photographing kids at weddings was one thing; conversing with them was quite another. 'Hello, Alessia. I'm very pleased to meet you.'

Alessia jerked her head away from Zach's shoulder and eyed her again, frowning a little.

Zach tickled her under the chin. 'Do you remember Olivia from Uncle Lucas's wedding? She took your photograph.'

Alessia began to writhe and giggle. Olivia took a few steps back. Watching Zach with his daughter, hearing the unfamiliar words pouring from his mouth so easily, was bringing her down to earth with a bump. She'd never thought about it before but of course he could speak Italian. He *lived* here. His *wife* had been Italian. Conscious suddenly of being the outsider, she turned away, hitched up the neckline of her top to cover her bare shoulder. Flirting, imagining—it had to stop here. He was embedded in a life that had nothing to do with her—a life she could never see herself being part of.

'Nonna!'

Alessia's cry broke into her thoughts and she turned to see an elegant woman walking down the grand hallway towards them.

'Lucia!' Zach shifted Alessia to one hip and held out his arm. 'Come meet Olivia.'

As she drew closer, Olivia could see strands of silver in the older woman's hair, sense the reticence in her slow smile. She was glad that Zach had warned her.

'Welcome, Olivia.' Lucia leaned in to air-kiss her cheek. 'Thank you for coming.' Another kiss. 'We are very grateful.' She stepped back, eyes searching Olivia's.

Olivia smiled. 'No, I'm the one who's grateful!' She couldn't read Lucia's expression and it was unnerving, so she tried to visualise the older woman as a reluctant wedding guest facing the camera. She'd found the trick to getting people on board was to be bubbly, to distract them in some way, so she stepped into the middle of the wide hall and looked up at the glittering chandelier suspended from the ceiling. 'This is astonishing!'

She'd been so mesmerised by Zach and Alessia that she hadn't properly looked at her surroundings, but now she took it all in. The patina of the wooden floor beneath their feet, the chalky yellow walls, the twin gilt-edged mirrors hanging over the console tables positioned on either side of the grand door. Beyond the vestibule where they were standing the floor of the wide inner hallway was laid with pale polished stone. The walls were hung with paintings and below the paintings there were more console tables, and occasional chairs.

When she finally looked round to smile at Lucia she wasn't faking her delight. 'It's so beautiful… Italy… Ravello! This house…everything! I'm over the moon!'

Lucia was looking at her with wide eyes and at the edge of her vision she could sense Zach stifling a laugh. Perhaps she'd overdone the enthusiasm, but then Alessia suddenly wriggled out of Zach's arms and came to stand by her side. She looked up, took a deep breath and said, 'This is *as-ton-ish-ing!*'

As Lucia and Zach burst out laughing, she breathed a sigh of relief. Never had she been so grateful to a child in all her life. She looked down at Alessia and grinned. 'I'm so glad you agree!'

Casa Isabella really *was* astonishing. As Zach showed her around, Olivia could feel herself falling in love with it. The rooms were large and airy, high-ceilinged, flooded with light. The décor was a mixture of antique and contemporary. What she liked most was that Casa Isabella felt like a home—a big home certainly, but every space was inviting.

Outside on the terrace, the view over the

grounds to the sparkling sea took her breath away. She wanted to explore the garden straight away, but Zach said they weren't finished inside yet. He led her back inside and along another wide hall on the ground floor.

'Your rooms are along here.'

'Rooms?'

'Of course! It's a small suite, a bit rustic—we haven't got as far as renovating this part of the house yet—but I think you'll be comfortable.' He opened a door off the hall. 'The kitchen's here.'

She stepped into a small, high-ceilinged room. It might have been a laundry room once, but now it was equipped with a fridge, a kettle, a two-ring hob and a microwave.

He smiled. 'It goes without saying that you can eat with us whenever you like...'

She tried to imagine eating dinner under Lucia's watchful eye. 'It's very kind of you to offer, but I'm sure your family time is precious.'

His eyes narrowed and he looked as if he was about to say something but then he stepped back into the hallway and opened a set of double doors on the opposite side. 'The rest of the suite is in here.'

She stepped through a small lobby and into a large comfortable sitting room. In one corner there was a desk with a computer and hard drives, but the rest of the room was set out for relaxing. A sofa and chairs were loosely arranged in front of a marble fireplace, lamp tables and other occasional tables scattered in between. The French windows overlooking the garden were open, white muslin curtains lifting in the breeze. She gazed at the view, all smiles. 'This is lovely.'

'It's a doer-upper, but I'm glad you like it. The bedroom's through there, and there's an en suite bathroom—it's old-fashioned but it works.'

She pushed open another set of doors and smiled again. The bedroom was spacious. The walls were whitewashed, yellowing in places, but the effect was charming. A huge antique bed was made up with white bedlinen, a blanket folded over the mahogany footboard. She noticed that her suitcase had already been brought in and left on a rack between a large wardrobe and a large chest of drawers. Everything in the room seemed large. She peeped into the en suite bathroom and smiled again. Claw-foot bath, huge porcelain sink and a separate shower recessed so deeply that there was no need for a screen.

She turned around. 'It's lovely, Zach.' The dark serious eyes she'd seen in the car had been replaced with twinkling blue ones and she was glad. Perhaps now that she'd cleared the hurdle of meeting Lucia he would relax. 'I don't know what I was expecting, but it wasn't this—I mean, a whole apartment to myself?'

'You'll need somewhere to hide from the mayhem.'

She sat down on the bed and gazed around the room. 'Is that what it's like?'

'It can get crazy sometimes. We've only got fifteen guest bedrooms, but we're filled to capacity every weekend and, as you know, weddings are demanding. There's all the coordination beforehand, then when the wedding party arrives it's busy. There's always an army of beauticians and hair stylists in tow, then caterers, florists—you know the score. After the wedding we have to keep going. Breakfasts, checking out the guests, arranging transport, room cleaning, maintenance, then it begins all over again.'

'Do you ever get time off?'

'Not much.'

She ran her hand over the quilt, felt its silky cotton softness. Eight-hundred thread count. *Nice.*

She looked up, found that he was watching her. Little butterflies started up in her stomach. 'So, why put yourself through it? Weddings, I mean. You could run yoga retreats instead—far less demanding!'

'Lower income too—this place costs a lot to run.' Suddenly, his eyes took on a faraway look and he turned away, walked to the window. For a few moments he gazed at the view. 'Actually, it's not about the money. It's because we fell in love...'

Silhouetted against the window, he cut a lonely figure. Olivia felt a shiver travelling up her spine, an urge to go to him, but instead she folded her hands in her lap.

'When we came to view this place we'd been looking for a going concern, a boutique hotel—something that we could just take over. But then this place came up. It was in a bad state. The interior was shot, the garden was a jungle. Everything was wrong with it, but it had good bones and as for the location... I remember we stood out there on the terrace as the sun was going down and it was romantic.' She could hear the smile in his voice, his evident fondness for the memory. 'Then Izzy looked at me and said, *"We should turn this into a wedding venue."* It was an inspired suggestion... I bought it the next day.'

Olivia imagined standing on the terrace with Zach, a fiery sunset over the sea, his body warm and close...but that was Isabella. He was in love with Isabella, he'd made his vows to Isabella, built a life and a home with Isabella.

Suddenly, he spun round and smiled. 'Impressive speech about gratitude, by the way. Not at all over the top.'

She could feel the warmth in his smile, felt that they really were becoming friends. She pulled a face and laughed. 'I was trying to be amenable. At least Alessia appreciated my performance.'

He laughed. 'Yes, thanks for that. *As-ton-ish-ing* is going to be her new favourite word.'

'Well, it's a good word.' She got to her feet and joined him at the window. 'It sums up Casa Isabella perfectly.'

CHAPTER THREE

FROM HIS OFFICE BALCONY, Zach could see Olivia working with the bride and groom in the garden. Over the hubbub of wedding guests on the terrace below, he could hear the occasional burst of laughter from the couple as she directed them through a walking sequence. She looked confident and relaxed, demonstrating to the bride how to hold the bouquet as she walked, adjusting the flower on the groom's lapel. He remembered the way she'd tidied his own buttonhole at Lucas's wedding, standing so close to him that he could smell the lingering fragrance of her shampoo. She'd taken him by surprise, or rather he'd taken himself by surprise, noticing things about her, like the way her smile reached all the way to her eyes, and the graceful way she moved.

He retreated into the room and poured himself a glass of water from a jug on the table. He'd thought she might be nervous about today—her first wedding at Casa Isabella—but he'd been watching her discreetly all day and she'd been every bit as polished and professional as he'd hoped. If she was nervous, she'd certainly kept it under wraps. He sipped from his glass, felt the cool liquid sliding down his throat. Soon her working day would be over. The wedding breakfast and speeches were finished. There was only the first dance left for her to shoot. Michele usually took a little break before photographing the first dance, but she was out there with the couple, taking pictures in the mellow evening light. Just yesterday she'd been telling him all about the golden hour, how it was the most beautiful light for romantic pictures, but as she'd been talking all he'd been able to think about was how much he liked the light in her eyes.

She was a breath of fresh air, a little breeze stirring his senses around, blowing through the veil of sadness that had settled over him since Izzy's death. As soon as he'd finished showing her around the house on the day she arrived, she was off exploring every inch of the grounds and formal gardens. All week she'd been out there, taking test shots, assessing the light at different times of the day.

Dedication!

Only this morning she'd suggested some adjustments to the ceremony layout on the terrace which would give her better shooting angles. 'The pictures are what the couple take away with them,' she'd said. 'We need to give them the best possible images, and that works for your business too because those pictures on your website gallery will help sell the venue.'

It was nothing he didn't know already, but although he was always busy and involved with things, of late he'd lost that intimate connection with the business that he'd had at the beginning. Olivia's energy and enthusiasm were challenging him, reminding him just how emptied out he felt.

Izzy's death would have finished him if it hadn't been for Alessia. Alessia was his reason for living, the reason why he'd needed to achieve Izzy's dream of turning this place into the perfect wedding venue. He was well aware that throwing himself into the renovation, driving himself day and night to push the project forward had been his way of coping with the grief. Eight months after Izzy's funeral, Casa Isabella had opened for business. Merrill Hotels now had a destination wedding venue in its portfolio, a database of eager couples looking for a romantic wedding venue in Italy. The first year had been a huge success. Five-star testimonials had led to a rush of forward bookings so that now he barely had time to breathe. When Olivia had asked him if he ever took time off, he'd wanted to laugh. Lucas's wedding had been his first weekend off in over six months.

Olivia threw herself onto the bed and exhaled a long, happy sigh. Her first solo wedding—in the bag! She smiled at the ceiling.

This morning, when she'd tapped on the bride's door, she'd been jittery with nerves, but after shooting the first few pictures the butterflies in her stomach had vanished. Now she was exhausted, but euphoric too. She was so glad she'd taken those last romantic pictures in the low light, got that little flare at the side of the frame. Stunning!

As she slipped out of her dress and pulled on her old jeans and a tee shirt, she was thinking about Ralph, how touchy and difficult he used to be during a wedding. After today, she could understand him a little better. The pressure had been relentless, not only because of the responsibility, but because she'd spent the day pushing herself, chasing the perfect shot— what Ralph used to call the money shot.

She freed her hair from its clip and shook it loose. She knew she should chill out, but she was buzzing. She simply had to download the pictures, take a look at what she'd got.

In the sitting room she switched on the computer. Zach had bought the best equipment for her, top quality hard drives, the latest graphics tablet. With sixteen hundred photographs to turn around in a week, she'd told him she would need a fast system and thankfully he'd listened. She started downloading the pictures then crossed to the French windows and flung them open. Instantly she could hear the muffled bass beat of the wedding band playing some lively number in the function room, snatches of chatter and laughter from guests relaxing on the terrace above. She stepped outside, breathed the fragrant evening air. The statues and fountain were lit up and there were more tiny lights twinkling amongst the leaves of the trees closest to the house. Everything looked magical. Isabella's dream brought to life.

Was running a wedding venue Zach's dream too? She couldn't help wondering…

He'd been on the go all day, on hand for the wedding planner, quietly making sure that everything was running smoothly. He seemed to drive himself hard, had admitted that he didn't take much time off, but it didn't make sense to her. The Merrill family was wealthy. There was the UK hotel chain and now this Italian wedding venue. She'd looked at the marketing brochures and the rate card. She knew how much it cost to have a wedding at Casa Isabella, and the place was booked solid! Even if her estimation of running costs was wildly inaccurate, she figured that Zach could easily afford to employ a manager. He employed other staff after all: a housekeeper, several cleaners, a secretary, two gardeners and a maintenance guy. Perhaps it was none of her business, but it bothered her that in the short time she'd been here she'd never seen him take Alessia out or play with her for more than five minutes at a stretch. It was clear that he adored his daughter, yet Alessia seemed to spend nearly all her time with Lucia. Olivia couldn't help feeling that if he didn't make time for Alessia now he would regret it later.

She massaged the back of her neck, felt memories unspooling. Her relationship with own father wasn't great, but at least she could look back at the happy times they'd shared... the way his eyes used to twinkle. *'Let's go adventuring, Liv!'* That always meant they were going to do something special—wild swimming, long walks, campfires and marshmallows. He was an ecologist—passionate about nature. He knew bird calls and the proper names of all the insects and plants. For the longest time she'd admired him. The way he stood out from the crowd—not just because of his height and his ponytail, but because he was outspoken. She remembered the primary school parents' night when he'd challenged her teacher about letting kids use plastic straws for a collage on the classroom wall, other parents and kids looking on, whispering.

She'd modelled herself on him. During a class session on religion and ritual across different cultures she'd proudly told the class that her parents weren't married, that marriage was an outdated ritual that had nothing to do with love and fidelity. She'd been defiantly vocal, just like he was—and then he'd left, moved to Wales.

She felt as if he'd hung her out to dry.

It hadn't helped that her three best friends all had parents who were happily married, ticking off anniversaries year after year. Celebration cakes, little weekend breaks, family get-togethers. No wonder she'd become fixated on a fantasy of perfection.

At university she'd tried to wean herself off the idea, tried to be more casual about relationships, but she'd failed. Now she knew her own mind. She wanted to do things by the book. A ring on her finger, total commitment, no loose ends. She wanted someone who would promise to love and cherish her for the rest of her life—someone who wouldn't leave like her father had. The trouble was, no one had ever come close.

'Hello?'

A voice from inside startled her. She listened again.

'Liv—?'

Zach!

She stepped back into her sitting room to find him standing in the doorway with a tray of food balanced on one arm and a bottle of wine in his hand. When he saw her, he lifted his eyebrows and put on a waiter voice. 'Room service for Olivia Gardner.' And then he came forward and set the tray and bottle down on a low table. He drew back to his full height and smiled. 'I also wanted to say thanks for doing such a great job today.'

He looked tired, she thought, strained around the eyes in spite of his smile. 'That's so nice of you, Zach, thank you.' She looked at the tray. It was filled with a selection of delicious-looking dishes from the wedding buffet, and a bowl of fat green pitted olives. All at once, she felt ravenous. She popped an olive into her mouth, then offered the dish to him. 'Will you join me?'

'I can't. I need to get back— Besides, I'm sure you could do with some peace and quiet.' She could see tension in his eyes and suddenly she really wanted him to stay, wanted to see him relax.

'Actually, I'm feeling a bit wired and I could use some company. I'm downloading today's pictures—if you stay you could look at them...'

His eyes darted to the computer. She could see he was tempted. She pushed a little harder. 'Look, I don't want to drink alone. Please, stay for a little while. I'm sure the wedding planner can cope without you and, to be honest, you look like you need a break.'

For a moment his expression clouded and she wondered if she'd crossed a line, but then slowly he smiled. 'I *would* like to see your pictures, and you're right! A glass of wine would really hit the spot right now. Is there a corkscrew in the kitchen?'

'Second drawer on the left.' He lifted an eyebrow and she laughed. 'The garden isn't the only place I recced thoroughly.'

He loved the photos and she was relieved; he'd brought her here to do this job after all. He liked the ceremony shots taken from the new angles, and he raved about the way she'd captured the atmosphere of the wedding—tiny details and big, happy smiles. He'd looked a little wistful when they got to the last photos of the couple in the garden at sunset and she wondered if he was thinking about Isabella.

Now she was curled up on the sofa with a second glass of wine, a little mellow buzz thrumming through her, and he was sitting in an armchair with his legs stretched out. He'd taken off his jacket and loosened his tie. She tried not to notice the dark hair at the base of his throat, the little hollow that she wanted to touch with her fingers and her lips. She imagined pulling his tie right off, reaching for the buttons of his shirt, undoing them one by one, feeling the delicious heat of his skin, the scent of him as she pressed her lips...

What was she doing? Zach Merrill didn't fit the profile of her ideal man. It didn't matter that his eyes seemed to run right through her, that she couldn't look at him without wondering what it would be like to touch him, but he could never be hers. He was still in love with his wife and he was her employer and he had a daughter *and* she was living under his roof alongside his mother-in-law. She forced herself to concentrate on his face.

He was looking around as if he was noticing the room for the first time. 'I haven't spent a lot of time in this part of the house. It's nice in here—like a little sanctuary.'

'That's it exactly! When I come in here and close the door, I forget I'm in a great big house. I love it!'

'What else do you love?' Smiling blue eyes. 'I'm curious.'

She felt herself blushing. 'You mean raindrops on roses, whiskers on kittens... That kind of thing?'

'It'd be a start!' He sipped his wine and suddenly his eyes grew more serious. 'What I mean is, here you are, helping me out, doing a fantastic job too, and I've suddenly realised that I don't know anything about you.'

She felt the breeze from the open window rippling over her bare arms, goosebumps prickling her skin. She didn't like talking about herself. With a camera around her neck she knew who she was, but without it, when the lens was focused on her, her instinct was to hide. She rubbed at her lower lip with her thumb, tried to sound casual. 'What do you want to know?'

He laughed. 'Don't look so terrified. We've both spent the day looking after people, being polite...careful about what we say. I just want to have a normal conversation, like, I don't know… Did you always want to be a wedding photographer?'

An image slipped into her head: herself clambering over a stile with her dad, big binoculars swinging from her neck. Suddenly she was laughing. 'No—for a while I wanted to be David Attenborough.'

His eyebrows lifted. 'You're a nature-lover?'

'I guess…' She smiled. 'My dad was—*is*—an ecologist. We used to go out a lot when I was little—birdwatching, deer-stalking. Lots of hiking! I had this huge pair of binoculars and I used to love looking through them, seeing things so close. It was like watching my own little wildlife film.'

'And now you spend your time looking through a camera lens. I can see a pattern.'

'Maybe I like spying on people—or maybe I like controlling the view…' She sipped her drink, lost herself for a moment. 'You can make things look perfect when you control the view.'

'So, you're either a spy or a control freak and your father is responsible?'

She shrugged. 'Well, you know what they say about formative influences—maybe I just like taking pictures.' He was looking at her, gently inquisitive, but she didn't want to talk about her dad. She remembered what she'd been thinking earlier, about Alessia. Perhaps she could steer the conversation in a different direction.

'Fathers and daughters—it's a special bond, don't you think?' She searched his eyes, wondering if he was hearing what she was saying to him. 'I see it at every wedding... *Who giveth this woman?* The little private looks, all that emotion.'

He looked down at his glass. Perhaps she'd struck a nerve. He got to his feet, retrieved the wine bottle from the table and topped up their glasses. 'I suppose so—but weddings are emotional events from start to finish. I can see *you* love it all.'

'Why wouldn't I? Weddings are very photogenic, especially in a venue like this.'

'So, you're all about the photo opportunities then?' He grinned. 'No misty eyes during the vows...?'

She felt a blush creeping over her cheeks. 'You were *watching* me during the vows?'

He was laughing now. 'I might have noticed you dabbing your eyes.'

She liked the way his face shone when he laughed, as if someone had switched a light on. She couldn't help smiling too. 'Okay, so I'll admit I get caught up in the ceremony. I find it moving, the idea of pledging yourself to another person for ever, being so sure that you've found the right one.' She sighed. 'Doesn't it get to you too?' His eyes darkened and instantly she regretted her question. 'I'm sorry—that was thoughtless—'

'It's okay.' He ran a hand through his hair, looked down at his glass. 'I don't usually watch the ceremony—but I do know this. When I saw Izzy walking towards me on our wedding day I felt...emotional...joyful. When you find the one you want to spend the rest of your life with, getting married feels like the most natural thing in the world. It was for me—I didn't have to think twice.' He looked up and suddenly his eyes were full of concern. 'Hey! You mustn't get upset.'

She hadn't noticed her eyes welling. The purity of his feelings had touched her, stirred an ache deep within her. It was as if he'd read out loud the script of her private fantasy. She wiped her tears away with her fingers and laughed to hide her embarrassment. 'I'm sorry...' She shook her head. 'How did we even start talking about this?'

'Binoculars, camera lenses, weddings...'

She shifted her position on the sofa and sipped her drink. 'Okay, change of subject. When you're not working, which is hardly ever, I've noticed, what do you like to do?'

He settled back in his chair and smiled slowly. 'I like playing the guitar.'

'You're a musician?'

He nodded, smiled sheepishly. 'A failed one. A million years ago I was in a band, but then I grew up.' He sipped his wine. 'I still dabble though. There's a bar in Ravello—I play most Thursday evenings—keeping my hand in.'

So, there was another side to Zach, something that was just him, something that wasn't connected to Casa Isabella. She felt as if she'd found a pearl in an oyster. 'That's amazing! What kind of music do you play?'

'Mostly classical these days, but sometimes I play with other guys, sort of improvised folksy stuff.'

'Could I come to watch you play?'

'Sure—if you want.' He looked shy suddenly. 'It's low-key, not very rock and roll.'

She smiled. 'I like low-key.'

He drained his glass and stood up. 'Okay then. It's a date—so to speak.'

She felt a blush warming her cheeks. Had she been too forward, inviting herself along? She hoped he was okay with it. Maybe he wouldn't want her there, invading his private world. If only she could see inside his head, know what he was thinking.

He was doing up his tie. 'I better get back.'

She rose to her feet, reached for his jacket just as he did. For a long moment she felt trapped in his gaze, felt the heat from his hands radiating through the fabric, and then somehow she made her feet move. She stepped back quickly, busied herself with tidying the used plates and glasses onto the tray. 'I'll wash these and bring them back tomorrow.' When she looked up again, she had to pretend that her heart wasn't beating like a drum. 'Thanks for the food and the wine—and the company.'

He seemed preoccupied as he shrugged into his jacket and walked to the door, but when he turned and smiled there was something in his eyes that made the breath catch in her throat. 'It was a pleasure. Goodnight, Liv.'

Zach walked slowly towards the reception hall. From the grand sitting rooms he could hear the hum of voices, the occasional burst of laughter—wedding guests enjoying time away from the dance floor. He envied Olivia, tucked away in her little suite. How peaceful it had felt there. It had been hard to make himself leave. That moment with the jacket, the way she'd been looking at him and the warmth of her hands so close to his, the sweet curve of her mouth. He'd felt a momentary madness, a desire to step closer and touch her lips with his own, and now he couldn't figure out if wanting to kiss someone who wasn't his wife was reprehensible or not. In two years he'd never so much as looked at another woman, but then there she'd been, at Lucas's wedding, Olivia Gardner! And he'd borrowed her pen and forgotten to give it back, and Michele had had his terrible accident and she'd stopped working for Holdsworth, and now she was here, under his roof, as if fate had somehow...

'Zach!'

Lucia was walking towards him, a look of slight consternation on her face. 'Alessia said you didn't read all of the story—'

'She fell asleep before the end.'

'Well, she must have woken up again.' Lucia sighed. 'The little monkey told me she was cross with you.'

He pictured his daughter's face, her cheeky smile, the way she frowned at him sometimes. 'She's always cross with me.'

Lucia's eyes grew serious. 'You need to spend more time with her, Zach.'

He pushed a hand through his hair and waited for two giggling guests go by. 'I know. Maybe tomorrow I'll take her somewhere.' He touched Lucia's arm. 'I'm sorry. I know you could do with a day off.'

'I don't mind looking after Alessia, you

know that, but she needs you, Zach. You don't have to take her anywhere. Just give her some of your time. That's all she wants.'

What had Olivia said? *Fathers and daughters—it's a special bond, don't you think?'* In the glow of the nightlight, he watched Alessia sleeping. Such thick dark lashes, just like Izzy's. He smoothed one of the little eyebrows with a gentle finger and she stirred for a moment before falling back into her dreams. He leaned in, kissed her forehead then quietly slipped from the room.

Lucia was right; he needed to spend more time with Alessia. He loved Alessia with all his heart, had never intended to step back, but in the months after Izzy's death, finishing the renovations and bringing her dream to life was all he could think about. If Alessia couldn't see her mother, he'd made up his mind that she would feel Izzy's presence everywhere: in the house, in the garden, all around. And then Casa Isabella had taken off and he'd been consumed by the demands of the business. Making it better. Making it even more perfect, always striving. Work had turned into a habit he couldn't shake because his feelings for Izzy were tangled up inside it.

He kept telling himself he'd get a manager,

but it hadn't happened yet. Perhaps if Lucia hadn't been a widow—perhaps if she hadn't been willing and able to step into the breach so completely—he would have been forced to balance his time better—would have been a better father.

He knew that it was time to cross that bridge, time to cultivate a special bond with Alessia before it was too late. She was growing up fast, becoming a proper little girl now. Soon she'd be laying down memories which she would take into adulthood, like Olivia's recollections of nature walks with her dad—big binoculars, little adventures. It was time for him to create adventures for Alessia.

He felt tired. He knew he ought to crash but instead he lifted his guitar off its stand and dropped onto the sofa. He tuned it by ear, little plucks of the strings until it sounded right, then absently he strummed a melody he'd been working on. He'd enjoyed being in Liv's apartment. She hadn't brought much with her, yet somehow she'd made the space her own... Flowers from the garden arranged in a jug on the mantelpiece, a scarf draped over a chair back, a small pile of books on a side table. And it had been nice just talking... He could tell that she found it hard to talk about her father and he was curious about that, but he hadn't wanted to ask…and then there'd been all that stuff about marriage and finding the perfect person, Liv almost in tears. But he hadn't minded talking about marrying Izzy. She'd been the love of his life.

He changed key, started playing the melody again. But it was confusing, the way he felt when Olivia looked at him, how he'd wanted to kiss her. Did it mean he was healing? Most days it didn't feel like that, but lately… He stilled his fingers, picturing Olivia earlier in the day, darting about with her cameras, so lively, so lovely in her summer dress. So off-limits.

His fingers started moving again. No matter how much he wanted to, he could never kiss her. She was here to work for him. Kissing her would be crossing a line—and what would he say afterwards? It was clear that she had romantic notions in her head, clear that she was looking for the kind of commitment he couldn't see himself giving again. Izzy had been the one and she was gone. He strummed a final chord then put the guitar back on its stand. He and Olivia would just be friends. That was as far as he would ever let it go.

CHAPTER FOUR

OLIVIA BLINKED AND pushed back her chair. She needed to take a break from the computer screen, stretch her legs. She supposed the wedding guests had all checked out by now. From mid-morning, through the open windows, she'd heard the sound of cars drawing up, the rise and fall of voices, doors sliding, tailgates banging and then it had gone quiet. Once again, clear as a bell, she could hear the tinkle and gush of the fountain in the garden, the chatter of birds in the trees.

She pushed her bare feet into her sandals and stepped through the French windows into the warmth of the afternoon sun. The informal garden at this side of the house was laid out in a series of shady rooms, like secret gardens, and she wandered from one to another until she came to a stone bench positioned to make the best of the sea view. She pressed her hand to the stone. It felt cool and inviting so she stretched out along its length and stared up at the infinite blue sky. For the hundredth time she thought about the night before, the way Zach had looked at her as they'd both held onto his jacket. He'd glanced at her mouth, a flicker of something in his eyes which had caused her heart to bang like a drum. Had he been thinking about kissing her?

She threw an arm over her face and closed her eyes. She'd thought about kissing him plenty of times, imagined what his lips would feel like on hers, but if it came to it, would she let it happen? *'I didn't have to think twice.'* That was what he'd said last night about marrying Isabella; it was obvious that he was still in love with his wife.

Suddenly the stone beneath her felt too hard and she pulled herself upright. He might have thought about kissing her, but it didn't mean anything. It couldn't mean anything because of Isabella. So…it must have been a reflex… because they'd been standing so close and because they'd had a glass or two of wine. The thrill of the moment tingled through her again. His eyes on her mouth, the ache in her veins…

She had to stop thinking about it! A casual fling with Zach, even if she was into that kind of thing, could only end in disaster. He was her employer and she needed this job, needed the portfolio she was going to create by working here. Jeopardising that would be madness.

She got to her feet, brushed herself down then paused. Even if Zach *did* like her, even if he wanted a proper relationship, would she dive in? As she turned it over in her mind, she was seized by an uncomfortable realisation. She couldn't help it—she wanted the fairy tale—the thrill of starting out together with everything ahead. Like that Carpenters' song about white lace and promises, new horizons...

Zach had had his beginning with Isabella. He had a daughter, a living, breathing part of Isabella who looked just like her mother he'd said... Olivia sighed. She couldn't see herself fitting in with a child, with Zach's readymade life. She'd always see ghosts in the shadows, so no matter how much she liked him, no matter how much she fantasied about kissing him, she could never let anything happen. Being his friend would have to be enough.

Slowly, she retraced her steps through the secret gardens then took a path which led to the formal garden. This was the garden with the best view of the sea. She gazed at the vast stretch of blue, watched the sparkling yachts and gleaming motorboats trailing white plumes of surf, their paths crossing and fading like chances. No wonder Zach and Isabella had wanted to buy this place—the location was perfect.

When she felt the sun burning her bare legs she turned back towards the house, pausing to take in the golden glow of its stone walls against the deeper greens of the surrounding trees and shrubs. She was about to walk on when she suddenly noticed that Lucia was waving at her from the terrace. She waved back, smiling, but as she got closer she realised that Lucia wasn't waving, she was beckoning. Perturbed, Olivia hastened up the three flights of stone steps to the main terrace, wondering why she was being summoned.

She'd barely spoken to Lucia since she arrived. She'd been busy, recceing the gardens, planning the best angles, taking test shots. She'd been terrified of making a mistake, of not being properly prepared for that all-important first wedding, and anyway, after Zach's warning, she'd decided it would be best to keep out of Lucia's way.

She cleared the final steps with a pounding heart, but when she looked across the terrace she couldn't help smiling. Alessia was splashing about in a little paddling pool, a big pair of green sunglasses perched on her nose. Lucia was hovering nearby with a towel over her arm and a slightly harassed expression on her face.

She looked rather overdressed for poolside duties, Olivia thought.

As she approached, Lucia looked up and beamed. 'Olivia! I hear the wedding went very well yesterday.' The older woman pulled her into a surprisingly warm embrace, kissed each cheek in turn. 'Zach told me you took wonderful photographs!'

'He said that?' It felt nice, hearing Zach's praise from Lucia's lips. 'I was a little nervous, to be honest, but it went well. The bride and groom were lovely—'

'Nonna! *Guarda cosa so fare?*' Alessia was pouring water out of a plastic teapot onto the terracotta setts.

Lucia turned and smiled. 'Very clever, my darling, but please speak in English—for Olivia.'

Alessia lifted her chin and peered over the sunglasses, which had slipped halfway down her nose, then she giggled and plunged her teapot back into the water.

Lucia turned back apologetically. 'I'm sorry to ask you, Olivia, and I wouldn't be asking at all if I hadn't seen you walking in the garden, but I'm meeting a friend in Ravello...'

That explained the outfit.

Lucia rolled exasperated eyes. 'Zach was supposed to be here but he had to take a phone call…and it's lasting a long time…' She lifted the towel off her arm, dangled it in her hands. 'So, I was wondering…'

Olivia could feel perspiration blooming on her back.

'Would you please stay with Alessia until he comes? It won't be long—it could be just for one minute, but I really have to go now…'

Lucia was holding out the towel, her eyes imploring. Olivia glanced at Alessia, felt her stomach kink. She had no experience of looking after small children. What if something happened whilst she was in charge? Lucia's eyes were warm, expectant, pleading.

Olivia nipped at her lower lip with her teeth and glanced at the pool again. *Six inches of water!* Alessia seemed to be perfectly happy, playing with a family of yellow ducks. Maybe Zach *would* be right down and perhaps babysitting Alessia would earn her some favour, ease Lucia's misgivings about her, whatever they might be. She sucked in a big breath and took the towel from Lucia's hands.

'Okay, I'll keep an eye on her until Zach comes back. It'll be…fun!'

Zach put down the receiver with a sigh. His father was hard to shake off when he was talking business, thought nothing of interrupting his son's Sunday afternoon to discuss marketing strategies and balance sheets. He was amazed that his father still had that fire in his belly, admired it in a way. Of late, his own fire had dwindled to barely a glow. He switched off his computer, tidied his papers into a pile. Lucia was going to be cross with him for taking so long, but this was how it always was for him. Work first!

As he walked through the house, listening to the echo of his disenchanted footsteps, he pictured himself at twenty-one, arriving in Rome with a rucksack on his back and a guitar case in his hand. He'd fallen in love with Italy during a family holiday and had always wanted to return, wanted to learn the language. So, after he'd finished his music degree, he'd bought a ticket…

He'd got a job in a pizza place, spent his evenings working in a bar, playing sometimes. In those days he'd fancied himself as Joe Satriani. He'd met other musicians, joined a band, spent two years gigging all over Europe. They'd got decent reviews, made enough money to keep body and soul together; they'd even started talking to record companies. They thought they were going places, believed they'd break through…but instead they broke up. They'd been in Naples when their charismatic lead singer suddenly announced he was going solo. Zach hadn't seen it coming. None of them had. They'd tried to find a new singer, but the glue was loosening. The band fell apart.

And then he'd met Izzy. Her family owned a restaurant in Naples and she'd been his waitress. He'd gone back night after night, just to see her, but soon he'd realised that he'd need to offer her more than his love, and his disillusionment with the music industry. He went back to England and joined the family business. His father had been delighted. Playing music was all very well, he'd said, but he thought Zach should have another string to his bow—his father used to like that joke! Ironically, another string to the Merrill Hotel group's bow was exactly what Zach achieved. He spearheaded a profitable new enterprise— Merrill Select—specialising in exclusive luxury boutique hotels. He was enjoying his success but Izzy owned his heart and soon his flying visits to Naples weren't enough. He'd come up with an idea. The Amalfi Coast was a burgeoning tourist spot—a prestige boutique hotel could do very well. It was the best compromise he could think of, running a Merrill Select hotel in Italy with Izzy. They'd been looking for a suitable place when they'd found Casa Isabella...

He'd traded music for the hotel business, traded the hotel business for an exclusive wedding venue, and then he'd lost his guiding star. If he felt adrift sometimes, perhaps it was understandable...

As he neared the terrace the sound of frenetic splashing and happy laughter interrupted his train of thought. He paused to listen. The voice he could hear with Alessia's wasn't Lucia's... He felt a smile coming as he softened his tread and moved closer. Beside a stone pillar he stopped and gazed across the terrace.

Olivia was standing in the paddling pool holding Alessia's hands. Alessia was jumping up and down, Olivia lifting her higher than she could jump on her own. They were both laughing and Alessia was shouting, 'Again! Again!' The area around the edges of the little pool was mottled and damp, littered with toys—yellow ducks, assorted buckets and a plastic teapot. It was a lovely scene, one he didn't want to interrupt, so he leaned against the pillar to watch. Olivia's legs were bare, glistening wet. There were splashes on her shorts and tee shirt, drops of water clinging to her face and hair. When Alessia stopped jumping Olivia helped her to sit down, then stepped out of the pool and knelt on a towel.

'Alessia, I'd like a nice cup of tea!' Olivia handed Alessia the plastic teapot and held out a little blue cup. 'Could you please pour me some?'

Alessia screwed up her face in concentration, dunked the teapot into the pool then looked up, spied him against the pillar and started to scramble to her feet. 'Papà!'

Olivia's hands shot out to steady her.

Zach wished he could have watched them for longer, but he'd been rumbled. He strode across the terrace. 'Hey! You look like you're having fun.'

Olivia looked up and smiled. 'We're having the best time ever, aren't we, Alessia?'

'Sì, sì, sì!'

Alessia reached for him and he lifted her into his arms. He felt the coolness of her little body, wetness from her swimsuit seeping into his shirt.

'Lucia had to go out.' Olivia was swiping water from her legs. 'She asked me to babysit.'

'I'm sorry—she should have brought Alessia to me.'

Olivia stood up straight and met his gaze with a little wide-eyed shrug. 'Alessia was playing! Lucia probably didn't want to spoil her fun. Anyway, I didn't mind.'

'Well, thank you—I appreciate it.' He sighed,

tidied wet strands of hair from Alessia's face then kissed her little nose. 'My father decided that today would be a good day to catch up on business. It's hard to get away once he starts talking.'

Olivia bent to pick up the ducks then launched them into the water. 'At least you still catch up—'

'*Paparelle!*'

Alessia was struggling in his arms so he put her down.

She squatted next to Olivia, picked up two of the ducks and pushed their beaks together. '*Bacio!*'

Olivia laughed, touched Alessia's shoulder. 'That's a kiss! Are the ducks kissing?'

Alessia giggled. 'Kiss!'

Light was bouncing off the water, reflecting on his daughter's face, dancing in Olivia's eyes. Watching them, Zach felt an unexpected swell of happiness. He was used to seeing Alessia with Lucia but, for some reason, the way she'd taken to Olivia pleased him beyond measure. He dropped down beside her and dipped his hand into the water.

'Do the ducks love each other?' Olivia was asking and Alessia returned a deep nod, her eyes dark and wise. She lifted one of the ducks to Olivia's mouth and Olivia laughed. 'You want me to kiss the little duck?'

Alessia giggled, pressed the duck's beak to Olivia's lips.

'Mwah!'

Alessia lifted the duck to his lips. 'Papà, you kiss the duck.'

Olivia was laughing at him now, eyes shining. He looked at Alessia then planted a kiss on the wet plastic beak. Alessia giggled again, her cheeks round and smooth as apples. Then he was laughing too. Perhaps the bridge he needed to build with his daughter wasn't so wide after all. He pulled her onto his lap and pressed his lips to her damp hair. When he looked up, Olivia was gazing at him softly.

She moistened her lips, shot him a little smile. 'I should go.'

Alessia wriggled backwards against his stomach, the sweet smell of her skin reminding him of vanilla. The warmth of the sun, the warmth of his daughter's body nestled against him felt so nice that he didn't want to spoil the moment with goodbyes, but how could he make Olivia stay? She was getting to her feet. He hesitated for a scant second then leaned in to his daughter's ear, stage-whispered, 'We don't want Liv to go, do we?'

Alessia tipped up her face to look at him

then scrambled off his knee and put her hand into Olivia's.

Olivia smiled down at her. 'But I have to go. I've got to work.'

Zach watched a familiar frown appearing on Alessia's face. It was the frown she used whenever he told her he was too busy to play.

She tugged on Olivia's hand. 'Why?'

Olivia looked at him, widened her eyes. She was trying not to laugh, he could tell.

'Because I work for your daddy and if I don't do my work he will be very sad.'

Zach dipped his hand into the pool again, ran his fingers back and forth. He could feel a smile growing on his lips. Using Alessia as a go-between was ridiculous. If he wanted Olivia to stay, there was only one thing for it. He cupped his hand to make a scoop and suddenly hurled a handful of water out of the pool. As it splattered over Olivia's legs, she shrieked, Alessia shrieked, then both of them laughed. Olivia fixed him with a look that made him jump to his feet and step back.

'Alessia! Can you please pass me the teapot? I think your daddy would like a nice cup of tea...'

Olivia pressed the towel to her face then blotted her hair. The puddles from their water fight

were evaporating quickly in the late afternoon
sun. She watched Zach drying Alessia, towel-
ling the little legs and arms, turning her this
way and that, pulling a little tunic dress over
her head. He was a good father, she could see
that. She looked away, gazed at the boats criss-
crossing the blue expanse of sea below. She
remembered days at the beach with her dad,
the way he'd throw a huge towel around her
when she came out shivering, enfold her in
his big, warm bear hug. And then he'd make
a fire on the beach by rubbing two sticks together, which was the coolest thing ever, and
he'd cook something he'd brought for them and
always there'd be toasted marshmallows afterwards. She smiled at the memory then let it
fade as she felt an incoming tide of pain.

'Who's hungry?'

She turned, saw that Zach had finished with
Alessia and was rubbing at his wet hair with
the towel. She couldn't resist a victory smile.
Her revenge for the splashing he'd given her
had been swift and satisfying. A pot of 'tea'
over his head, with Alessia laughing so much
she'd got the hiccups. Then there'd been chasing, water being flung from buckets, a game
of catch the duck: total mayhem. Good fun.
But she couldn't stay—she hadn't meant to
stay this long.

She slipped on her sandals. 'Thanks, but I should go.'

He dried his face and smiled. 'Eat with us, Liv. Please… It's nothing fancy—just pizza. You can work later…'

She could see in his eyes how much he wanted her to stay, but there was something else too, something in his gaze that was making the ground shift beneath her feet. She felt her stomach tilt. The problem was that she *wanted* to stay, *wanted* to share whatever it was they'd been sharing all afternoon but she was torn, confused by a blurring of lines which she thought she'd drawn in permanent ink.

Suddenly an irresistible little hand pushed its way into hers. She looked down to see Alessia looking up at her through thick, thick lashes. 'Don't you like pizza?'

She smiled and threw Zach a helpless look. 'I like it if it doesn't have pineapple on it.'

Zach flung his arms out, mimicked a strong Italian accent. 'Theze eez *It*-aly! Pineapple is for-*beeden*.'

He looked so comical that she couldn't help laughing. She looked down at Alessia, squeezed the little hand. 'Okay, in that case I'm in!'

Zach's ground-floor suite was located at the opposite end of the house to hers. There was a large open-plan kitchen/sitting room, flooded with light from two sets of French windows. The décor was neutral, the furniture comfortable, but Olivia got the impression that it was a work in progress. Bare wires poked through one of the walls in the kitchen—*'Waiting for wall-lights,'* he told her. There was a collection of pictures propped against the wall in the sitting room—*'Waiting to be hung,'* he said. She noticed his guitar, sleek as an amber jewel, parked on a stand in the corner.

Alessia took her hand, tugged her through the apartment to her own little bedroom. In contrast to the living area, Alessia's room was finished to the highest degree: brightly painted walls in a delicious shade of mango, colourful pictures, a blue toy box and bookcase, a white wardrobe and chest of drawers. Alessia shifted a row of teddy bears so that Olivia could sit on the bed then she knelt in front of the toy box, pulling out dolls and plastic ponies, chattering away, half to herself and half to Olivia.

As she looked around, Olivia could feel Isabella…could read the past as if it had been written on the wall. They must have been working on the renovation, discovered that they were expecting a baby. She could hear Isabella's voice: *'There's mess everywhere, Zach. We need this room to be perfect for the baby…'*

A photo frame on the bedside table caught her eye and she picked it up.

Isabella!

A lovely face framed by straight dark hair, cheekbones defined by the makings of a smile. Her eyes sparkled with a warm, mischievous light, as if she had a secret she was dying to tell.

Olivia stared at the photograph, losing herself in the eyes of the woman who'd captured Zach's heart, until a clatter of toys on the floor jerked her out of her trance and hurriedly she put the frame back.

She watched Alessia trotting a pair of white ponies with long pink manes across the floor, making little clicking noises with her tongue. She *was* like her mother—would look more and more like Isabella as she grew up.

Olivia wondered what Zach had told her. *Mummy's in heaven...?* It was what she would say if Alessia was hers. *Mummy's in heaven but she's watching you all the time, sending her love to you on...sunbeams.* Something like that...something Alessia could see.

She heard approaching footsteps then Zach appeared in the doorway, waving a bottle. 'Glass of wine?'

Alessia looked up, carried on clicking her tongue.

'Sounds great!' Olivia put the jumbled teddy bears back into line then stood up. When she caught Zach's eye she could see amusement on his face and she felt her cheeks creasing into a smile. 'What? It's how I found them.'

He shook his head a little and smiled, then dropped to his haunches. 'Alessia, why don't you bring Poppy and Wizard into the sitting room for a gallop?'

Alessia rocked back on her heels, pushed the hair out of her face. 'Okay.'

Olivia followed Zach through the apartment. She liked the way he walked, the way his hair grazed his collar at the back of his neck, dark and soft. She liked the shape of his shoulders, broad, dependable-looking. Behind her, she could hear Alessia's tongue still clicking furiously and it was hard not to laugh. She liked Alessia, found her sweet and comical. That she could find a child fascinating was a revelation. She'd never spent a lot of time with small children. As an only child, she'd been surrounded by adults most of the time. She had a vague recollection of the kids at nursery school, but that was different—they'd all been kids together then. Alessia was the first youngster she'd spent proper time with, and she'd enjoyed every moment.

In the kitchen she watched Zach checking

the temperature of the oven and deftly adjusting the shelves. She was so busy admiring the
graceful way he moved that it took her a moment to notice the little piles of neatly sliced
onions and peppers, the stack of grated mozza-
rella and thinly sliced Italian sausage arranged
on the large marble island unit. Two large pizza
bases were arranged on baking trays—floury.
Freshly made!

'You *make* your own pizza from scratch?'

He poured the wine and handed her a glass,
a mischievous glint in his eye. 'Yeah! Doesn't
everyone?'

She laughed. 'No—o!'

'To be fair, I don't make it often these
days—' He picked up his glass, touched it to
hers. 'But since Alessia woke me up at stupid o'clock this morning I thought I'd make
some dough—to get into her good books. She
loves my pizza!' He sipped his wine, smiling.
'It's not a big ask. I've had plenty of practice.
I worked in a pizza place for a while, when
I first came to Italy.' He parked his glass on
the side, started spooning tomato sauce over
the bases and smoothing it out with the back
of the spoon, then he looked up. 'That was in
Rome…a long time ago.'

The intensity of his gaze was disconcert-
ing. She groped for the backrest of a tall stool,

pulled it out and seated herself as casually as she could manage. 'Were you studying Italian? Is that why you came here?'

He scattered toppings over the pizzas with a practised hand. 'No! I studied music, but I've always loved Italy and I wanted to learn Italian, so after my degree I came over…and, apart from a shortish stint in England, I've been here ever since.' He pulled open the oven door and threw the two tins inside, then picked up his glass and drank. 'Right! There's a bowl of salad in the fridge. If you could grab it and give it a toss that would be great. Dressing's over there.' He smiled. 'I'm going to get Alessia washed and then we can eat.'

'So, what's the story with your dad?'

Olivia spluttered into her glass and swallowed hard. She was glad that he was putting the leftover salad into the fridge and couldn't see her reaction. The remark about her dad had fallen from her mouth accidentally when he'd been telling her about his own father. She thought he hadn't noticed, was glad that he hadn't picked up on it, but he'd obviously been biding his time, waiting for the right moment to come back to it. Was there ever a right moment for that conversation? Fathers… Daughters… She glanced at Alessia, who'd fallen asleep on the sitting room sofa—out for the count. 'I… Erm—'

Zach was leaning over the island unit now, refilling her glass. 'I'm sorry if that was a buzzkill—you don't have to answer.'

There was a gentle light in his eyes and for a moment she felt the tug of it, as if he was guiding her to a safe haven, a place where she could open up and talk. She pressed the tip of her tongue against her teeth. The thing was, her feelings about her family were such a muddle, she wouldn't know where to begin. *No!* She'd have to give him the brush-off.

She reached for her glass, took a hefty sip. 'It's nothing really. We used to get on; we don't any more.' She'd managed to sound blasé, but inside she was breathing through the pain she felt, consciously smothering the little judder in her heart.

Zach put the bottle down and settled himself onto a chair. He was looking at her intently. She looked away, fingered the stem of her glass. She wanted to drink the lot, but it would only make her feel worse.

He sighed. 'I shouldn't have asked—I'm sorry. It's just that when we were talking last night I got the impression you were close to your dad, so I was surprised about what you said this afternoon, about not catching up with him…'

'It's the way things go sometimes…' Olivia sipped her wine again, held it in her mouth for a few seconds before swallowing. What did it matter anyway? Maybe telling Zach about her dad would make him see how important it was to stay close to Alessia, to not let work come between them. As long as she kept her tone matter-of-fact, she'd manage—it was only conversation, after all.

She looked up, met his gaze squarely. 'I told you that Dad's an ecologist. What I didn't say was that he's rather unusual.' *Breathe.* 'Both of my parents are unusual.' She gave a little shrug. 'Mum used to wear these long skirts, jumpers knitted by yaks—are you getting a picture?'

Zach nodded.

'And Dad's tall. He's got a ponytail and big feet in big boots. You might say that my parents stood out in a crowd.' She sipped her wine again. 'They never got married. They didn't see the point! They weren't into all that. They were into conservation. When I was growing up, Dad was involved in a lot of environmental campaigns. He thought nothing of berating my teachers for "ecologically unsound" decisions in the classroom. He tended to draw attention to himself—and there was a knock-on effect…'

Zach's eyebrows lifted in a question and she forced herself to continue.

'At school I used to get teased a bit—nothing drastic—but I was marked out because of my parents, and…well, because of myself too. Back then I was just like my dad. I was outspoken. I challenged people about things, set myself up for—' she fingered her glass through a hazy memory of taunting faces '—but you know I was okay with it because I was proud of Mum and Dad. I respected them. Dad was my absolute, total hero—better than all the other dads by a mile.' She could feel a bubble building in her chest but Zach was looking at her, eyes so blue and clear and kind that she wanted to go all the way. She swallowed hard.

'So…not long after my thirteenth birthday, Dad came into my room one morning and told me he was leaving…he said he was moving to North Wales… He'd been offered this Field Ecologist's job, something that would really make a difference, he said, and he couldn't turn it down…

'I didn't understand why he kept saying that *he* was leaving, not *we*.' She could feel a hot glaze of tears at the edges of her eyes and swallowed hard again. 'But you see that was the second bombshell. Unbeknown to me, their relationship had *run its course*— that's what he said!' She blinked, felt a wet trickle sliding down the side of her face. 'Then Mum came in. She said it had been a mutual decision. She didn't want to move to Wales. She said that she and Dad would still be friends…that there was nothing for me to worry about—' The empathy she could see on Zach's face was suddenly too much to bear. She closed her eyes, swallowed the lump that was thickening in her throat. 'But there was! Because for years I'd been telling everyone at school that marriage was pointless. I was very vocal about it…so you see…' she dropped her face into her hands '…lots to worry about.' Tears were sliding freely down her cheeks now, winding through her fingers, and she didn't want to be crying like this in front of him but she couldn't stop. She tried to speak, big wet gulps of words. 'I felt—so—stupid.' And then, through a haze of tears, she sensed him standing, moving towards her.

'Liv. You were thirteen.' His hand was on her shoulder, he was coaxing her up, smoothing the hair away from her face. 'I can't watch you crying and not put my arms around you.'

And then she was melting against him, drawn into his warmth, and it felt like hours before the tears began to subside. His hand was gentle at her back, a little rigid at first, then softer until she could feel a gentle pressure from his fingertips. She could feel the damp crush of his shirt against her cheek, his heart beating, and slowly, almost imperceptibly, a steady heat began to flow through her veins, a new kind of awareness. He was feeling it too, she could tell. The moment was heavy, so heavy that it felt like a weight pressing down on her. He shifted on his feet and she sensed him looking down, waiting... For what—for her to lift her face? The thought of it made her dizzy.

'Papà...'

'Alessia!' He breathed his daughter's name and Olivia felt his arms slackening around her, a cool invasion of air between them as he stepped back. He was looking at her, a strange hazy light in his eyes. 'Are you okay?'

She swiped at her eyes and her cheeks. 'Yes—I'm sorry.' Her words were tumbling out in a rush. 'Thank you for holding—I must look a state—I should go.'

He put a hand on her arm. 'You don't look a state and you don't have to go—there's more to talk about.'

'Papà, *dove sei?*' The voice from the other room was sleepy.

'I'm right here, Alessia. I'm coming!'

He was still holding her in his gaze, a weight of kindness in his eyes that was making her bubble up again and she couldn't bear it. She took a step towards the door. 'Go to her. I'm fine, really. You don't have to worry about me.'

CHAPTER FIVE

OLIVIA SUDDENLY REALISED that she'd been staring at the same photograph on her computer screen for ten whole minutes. She pushed her chair back, walked to the open windows and looked out. Today the view reminded her of a holiday postcard: harsh light, saturated colours, zero charm. She slumped against the casement, felt the restless curtains brushing her bare feet.

Zach had come to see her the morning after her meltdown. She'd smiled, apologised for crying all over his shirt then told him she was really busy. She hoped he could see that she didn't want to talk. She couldn't. Not until she'd untangled the knot inside her head. It was what she'd been trying to do for the past three days, but everything was mixed up: feelings about her dad, feelings about Zach and Alessia. For every thread she managed to straighten out there was another one twisting itself even tighter.

Perhaps she should have left the terrace

the moment Zach arrived that day, but she'd been enjoying herself with Alessia more than she could ever have imagined and Zach had seemed so pleased, had looked at her with such a happy light in his eyes that she couldn't bring herself to walk away. She'd been mesmerised by him, by how he was with Alessia. The way he'd drawn Alessia into his lap, the way he'd kissed her head…it had made her think about her dad, churned her up about it all.

Her mum used to smile at her, tell her she was a daddy's girl. She loved her mum but spending time with her dad always felt special. He was her best friend! She closed her eyes, trying to see beyond…

Zach smoothing Alessia's wet hair away from her face, kissing the plastic duck because she wanted him to… *'Why don't you bring Poppy and Wizard into the sitting room for a gallop?'* He knew the names of Alessia's little ponies…because he was interested…because he loved her…because to him Alessia was the most special little girl in the world…

Olivia sank to the floor and wrapped her arms around her knees. She could feel the ache of tears behind her eyes again. Her dad had been like that…with her. She was an only child, his only daughter… Had he found *her* interesting? Had he wanted to spend time with *her* as much as she wanted to spend time with him? It had never occurred to her before, but had she been *his* best friend too?

And now she remembered the pain in his eyes when she told him he'd let her down. He'd sat on her bed, reached for her hand but she'd pulled it away. 'Liv, I'm moving out, that's all. I'm not abandoning you… There's a room for you in my new place…you're still my girl. Didn't I bring you up to be a free spirit?' She hadn't been able to speak, to fit words to the confusion in her head, so she'd twisted her fingers in her lap and stared at the carpet.

He'd put a hand on her shoulder. 'I'm not letting you down. I love you. I'm here for you. I'll always be here for you… But sometimes life leads you onwards, you know. You can go with it or you can stick…' She'd felt the pressure of his fingers on her shoulder, a little squeeze. 'I have to go with it… I thought you of all people would understand.'

She'd tried to understand but her relationship with him had changed after that. There was something unhealed between them, something she couldn't push past. Her role model, her hero, had flown off into the sunset to fight the good fight somewhere else. He'd found something more important than his family. More important than *her*. That was the way it had felt to her thirteen-year-old self.

The start-up kick of a lawnmower broke into her thoughts—the gardeners getting everything ready for the next wedding. She let her knees drop out and sat cross-legged. She wished she hadn't told Zach about her dad. Digging through old memories, delving into deeply personal stuff was tipping the scales too far. He was her boss! She pictured the mischief on his face as he'd hurled water at her legs, felt a smile tugging at her lips. Okay, maybe he was also a friend, becoming one anyway. But then, when he'd been holding her, there'd been that moment…

She got to her feet, poured herself a glass of water. In a moment of weakness he might have given her the impression that he wanted to kiss her…but maybe she'd misconstrued things. She'd been upset and it had felt so nice being held in his arms, all warm and safe, and there'd been that lovely subtle scent of his cologne, the rise and fall of his ribcage, the steady beat of his heart… Easy to get things muddled up with all that going on. Muddles and tangles and confusion, Zach whirling around in it. She couldn't stop thinking about him, couldn't stop wondering why his arms had felt like home when the home she'd sold herself looked so different.

She sipped her water.

Free spirits—that was how she'd seen her parents when she was growing up, but after her dad left she'd questioned the whole ethos. Suddenly all that freedom seemed like a messy way to live, and she didn't want messy. A clean start with someone demonstrably committed to her—that was what she'd set her heart on. Good times, bad times, making a home and having a family, growing closer, working things out, weathering the storms. With Zach, she'd be stepping into Isabella's shoes and maybe she wouldn't fill them properly. Maybe she wouldn't live up to *his* expectations and he'd end up disappointed, the way she'd been disappointed in her dad. She pressed the cold glass to her forehead. She was getting ahead of herself, thoughts running away with her, getting tangled up again. *Stop it!* Nothing had happened with Zach.

As she sat down at her desk and reached for the computer mouse, Alessia's face shimmered in front of her eyes, trotting the little ponies, tongue clicking nineteen to the dozen... She sighed. Any kind of relationship with Zach Merrill was bound to be complicated, and she wasn't at all sure that she had the heart for complications.

* * *

Olivia pulled the USB stick out of the computer and fitted it into its box. *Done!* Eight hundred wedding photos edited, processed and ready to send to her first bride and groom! She wanted to run upstairs and tell Zach, but she could hardly do that when she'd been avoiding him for the past three days. Her jubilation evaporated instantly. Hiding away had felt right at the time but, thinking about it now, she wondered if her behaviour had been a little childish. What must he have thought when she turned him away from her door? Had he been hurt?

The sound of voices broke into her thoughts—a familiar little giggle then a knock. *Alessia!* Her mouth went dry. *Zach?*

She hurried to the door but, when she opened it, it was Lucia who was standing there, holding Alessia's hand. Alessia was jiggling up and down and as soon as Lucia let go of her she rushed forward and wrapped her arms around Olivia's legs.

'Well, this is a lovely surprise!' Olivia bent down, hugged the little body, kissed the top of her head. Alessia's hair smelt sweet and clean. She had the urge to lift her up and cuddle her in, but Lucia was watching, waiting to talk to her.

'Hello, Olivia. I'm sorry if we are disturbing you but Alessia wanted to say hello.' The older woman kissed her on both cheeks then stood back and smiled. 'We haven't seen you in the garden for a few days. You're just like Zach—always working.'

Olivia felt her heart skip at the mention of Zach's name. 'I've been busy. Erm…would you like to come in?'

'If it's okay, we'll come in for just a minute.' Lucia smiled apologetically. 'Alessia wanted to see your room…'

'Well, I suppose that's fair.' Olivia stepped aside for Lucia to enter. 'Alessia did show me *her* room, after all—' For a moment her words seemed to hang in the air above them and she faltered. Did Lucia know that she'd spent an evening with Zach and Alessia? *Probably! Definitely!* She sucked in a deep breath and followed Lucia into the sitting room, Alessia dancing and hopping at her heels. 'Can I get you some tea, or some lemonade?'

'No, thank you.' Lucia was looking around then met her eye and smiled. 'Are you happy down here? It's a quiet part of the house…'

'I love it, maybe because it *is* so quiet.'

Lucia's eyes glowed warmly. For some reason Olivia found it hard to hold her gaze so she glanced at Alessia, who was examining her computer desk from a safe distance. She'd clearly been instructed not to touch anything. When she turned back to Lucia, she suddenly noticed the older woman's well-fitting white dress with navy topstitching, the red glossy nails, freshly painted. She wondered if Lucia was going on a date. It was hard not to smile at the thought of it. 'You look very nice, Lucia. Are you going out?'

The older woman coloured slightly. 'Yes—I have…a thing…in town—'

Definitely a date!

'Is Alessia going too?'

Lucia shook her head. 'No…she's staying here… Maria's going to keep an eye on her until Zach's finished his meeting with the accountant.'

Olivia pictured Maria, the housekeeper, a bustling, slightly breathless middle-aged woman who always seemed to be busy with laundry. Would Maria have time to play with a three-year-old child? It seemed unlikely, whereas Olivia herself happened to be free.

Olivia glanced at Alessia, who was now peering closely at the scarf she'd draped over the back of a chair—a present from her dad—navy silk printed with bumblebees and dragonflies. She smiled. 'Lucia, would you like me to look after Alessia?'

Lucia's eyes widened. 'No, no, no! I wouldn't want to impose—'

'But I'd like to—I've just finished editing my first wedding and I was about to go out for a walk.' She turned to Alessia. 'Would you like to go for a walk with me, Alessia? We could go adventuring...'

All smiles, Alessia bounded over and reached for her hand. '*Sì!*'

Olivia laughed. 'I understand *that* word.'

Lucia smiled hesitantly. 'Well, if you're sure... it would be very nice for her.' She lifted an eyebrow. 'She seems to have taken to you, Olivia.'

Olivia grinned, squeezed Alessia's little hand in hers. 'And I've taken to her too.'

Lucia beamed. 'I'll tell Maria then.' She turned to Alessia. 'Now, be a good girl for Olivia.'

'*Sì*, Nonna.'

'Oh, and Olivia? Could you please tell Zach that I'm having dinner out, but I'll be back before he has to go?'

'Of course.' Olivia wondered where Zach was going. Perhaps he had a date. A little knot started twisting in her stomach just thinking about it. She was so distracted that she didn't notice Lucia walking towards the door until the older woman turned around and looked at her. It was a long look, wistful.

'You know, in this light you remind me a little of my daughter.'

Olivia gripped Alessia's hand. She didn't know how to respond.

Lucia smiled. 'I hope you have good adventuring, as you call it.' She winked at Alessia and then disappeared through the door.

For a long second Olivia didn't move, then suddenly she became aware of Alessia staring up at her. She looked down, caught a fleeting impression of Zach in Alessia's eyes which took her by surprise. She smiled. 'Shall I bring the camera? I could take some nice pictures of you for your daddy and for Nonna—would that be nice?'

Alessia nodded enthusiastically.

'Okay then, let's go!'

The light had mellowed and the day looked softer now, the colours richer. Olivia wanted to explore the outer reaches of the property, but soon discovered that walking with a three-year-old required an unhurried pace. Alessia kept stopping to examine the smallest things: a fallen leaf with curly edges, a hairy caterpillar looping along the ground… But it was nice listening to Alessia's chatter, pointing things out to her. Olivia realised how often she was repeating her dad's words, telling Alessia the proper name for the cloud they could see, or the name of a flower...smothered memories unfolding like petals as they walked.

By the time they reached the dark hush of the olive grove, Alessia was flagging. Olivia picked her up, felt the little arms snaking around her neck. 'Shall we have a rest?' Alessia nodded and suddenly she felt guilty for bringing her this far. There was an old bench under a nearby tree and she carried Alessia there, put her down then sat down beside her. Within moments, Alessia was scrambling onto her lap. For a second Olivia hesitated, then she slipped her arms around her. It felt nice, a little strange.

She'd started noticing things about Alessia that reminded her of Zach—like the way she walked and the way she looked when she was concentrating on something. As she held Alessia, she got the strangest feeling that she was holding Zach too, and it felt like a little release, like an outlet for all the confusion in her head. She lowered her face, felt the softness of Alessia's hair against her cheek and pulled her a little closer.

Zach switched off his computer and stretched. His meeting with the accountant had felt interminable. He'd struggled to concentrate because he'd been thinking about his set for the evening. Playing in the bar was the highlight of his week, the only time he could forget everything and lose himself in music. He got to his feet and walked over to the window. The view was spectacular. He could see the formal garden with the craggy Amalfi Coast beyond—blue sea and sky—but he wasn't really looking at it. He was wondering what to do about Olivia.

He hadn't seen her all week and that was fine. He understood. If she didn't want to talk about things, he could respect that. But he couldn't help wondering if she was avoiding him because of the other thing that happened—or rather the thing that hadn't happened. It had confused him too, sent his own thoughts wandering into unfamiliar territory.

Their afternoon by the paddling pool had reminded him of how joyful life could be. Alessia and Olivia seemed to have an easy compatibility and he'd been drawn into it, hadn't wanted Olivia to leave because it felt right. It felt like the way things were supposed to be.

When Izzy died, Alessia had barely started walking so they'd never had that kind of family time together. The paddling pool afternoon had been a new experience for him, and he'd loved every minute of it. He could still hear Alessia's laughter as Olivia poured the water over his head, still see the way Olivia had been looking at him, her eyes shining with mischief. And then later when she'd been crying, and he'd held her, there'd been that moment when he'd started noticing how good her body felt pressed against his, and he'd realised how much he missed being warm and close to someone who was not his daughter. He'd wanted to tilt Olivia's face to his, kiss her, lose himself in her warmth and her softness.

He didn't know what to make of his thoughts. For so long he'd been putting one foot in front of the other, not really thinking about anything except achieving Izzy's dream. Working long hours, not spending enough time with his daughter. And now Olivia was here, bailing him out, messing with his head. Was there a way to put things straight, to draw a line in the sand? It should be easy. Liv was working for him, which meant that their relationship ought to be strictly professional, but she was living in his house, and Alessia liked her. *He* liked her—and he got the feeling that she liked him too.

He walked slowly out of his office and closed the door behind him. Avoiding each other wasn't going to solve anything. He needed to see her, be friendly with her. That was the only way he'd be able to put things back on the level. She'd told him she wanted to watch him play at the bar. Maybe he could ask her if she still wanted to go. Hopefully, if he made it sound casual, it would break the ice.

He was heading down the stairs when two figures caught his eye through the half-landing window. One tall, one small, walking down the cypress avenue.

Olivia and Alessia!

He wondered where Lucia had gone, hoped that Olivia wasn't feeling put upon—he hadn't brought her here to be his daughter's babysitter. He took the stairs two at a time, plunged through the grand doors and hurried down the stone steps.

'Papà!'

Alessia started running towards him, a happy smile on her face. 'Hello, monkey!' He scooped her up then turned to Olivia and smiled cautiously. 'Babysitting again?' She looked pale, he thought, a little tired.

'Lucia had a…thing…in town.' He saw a hesitation in her smile, which bothered him. 'Maria was going to mind Alessia but, since I was going for a walk anyway, I offered to take her with me.' She stepped closer, touched Alessia's cheek. 'We had a nice time, didn't we?' Alessia nodded, let her head drop against his. Olivia looked at him apologetically. 'She's tired. I probably walked too far... I'm not used to kids.'

'You could have fooled me!' He stroked Alessia's hair. 'You're really good with her.'

'That's because she's adorable. She's easy to lo—' She stepped back, fiddled with the camera around her neck. 'I was going to take some pictures, but it never happened...' A smile played on her lips. 'We found a butterfly...'

'And some ants, Papà!'

Olivia laughed, warm light filling her eyes again. 'Yes! Lots of ants—and we sang the song!'

'The song?'

Olivia giggled, looked at Alessia and started to sing. '"Now the army ant did say..."'

Zach felt his cheeks creasing into a smile as Alessia joined in.

'"I don't want to march all day..."'

As the words of the old song came back to him, he couldn't resist singing too. '"I want to dance not drill, tap my feet until, I'm a true formicidae."'

He was laughing hard now; so were Olivia and Alessia. When Alessia warbled the last line again, he laughed even more, joined in with the next verse, widening his eyes, acting the fool, being utterly, joyfully silly. When he noticed that Olivia had stopped singing, he looked around then laughed all over again. She was standing a little distance away, taking pictures.

'Now *that* was a golden moment!' She widened her eyes, shot him a cheeky smile. 'I couldn't resist.'

It felt so good to see her, so good to see her smiling again that Zach only realised he was staring when she looked down, clicked a little switch on the camera. She took a step backwards then lifted her hand. 'Oh! Lucia said to tell you she was having dinner out but she'll be back before you have to go…'

For some reason his pulse was climbing. 'Right. Thanks…' She was gazing at him and he could tell she was about to walk away. He'd intended to throw the bar invitation into the conversation casually but the ant song had stolen his thunder. Now he was going to have to invite her more formally. He drew in a breath. 'I'm playing at the bar tonight… I told you about it, remember?'

She lifted her chin. '*That's* where you're going!'

'Where else?' He smiled. 'Do you still want to come?'

Her expression softened. 'Well, I *have* finished editing the Hadleigh wedding so I'm free...'

He could feel Alessia's fingers twirling in his hair, hear her giggling in his ear. 'So that's a yes?'

Olivia smiled, eyes full of light. 'Yes—I'd like that, thank you.'

'Great! We'll leave at half-eight. I'll meet you out here.' Alessia's fingers were raking his hair upwards now. He grinned. 'That's assuming my hairstylist has finished by then.'

Olivia pulled back the doors of her wardrobe and gazed at the contents: three summer dresses suitable for wedding days, a pair of faded jeans, two pairs of smart shorts, one pair of denim cut-offs, assorted tops, a pair of white crops and a denim jacket. Three pairs of sandals and a pair of blue sneakers were arranged at the bottom. She hadn't brought much, intending to buy anything else she needed locally, but that hadn't happened yet. She ran a hand over the hangers. The choice of outfit was important. She wanted to look nice, but not done up.

Seeing Zach again, singing the silly song, laughing together—it had felt so right. She'd missed his smile, the kindness in his eyes... She reached for the white crops and a black

V-necked tee shirt. Going to see him play this evening, spending time with him on her own would be good for her, would give her a chance to redraw the boundaries in her head. She laced up her sneakers, pulled on the denim jacket. She considered lip gloss, decided against. It was going to be hard, but somehow she had to plant Zach firmly in the friend zone.

As she walked through the house she felt a little surge of happiness. Getting away from Casa Isabella for the evening was just what she needed. A change of scene. She was dying to see Ravello, dying to see Zach in a different environment, playing his guitar. He'd looked a little wistful when he told her he played, called himself a failed musician. He'd studied music so he must have been serious about it once, but now he was running a wedding venue and playing in a bar once a week…

'Hi!'

She stopped in her tracks. He was walking along the hall towards her, guitar case in hand. He was wearing jeans, not chinos, and the kind of tee shirt women like to steal: faded, butter-soft. Sexy. She swallowed hard, reminded herself about the friend zone. 'Hi!'

He smiled. 'Ready to go?'

There was an energy about him—like electricity. He couldn't wait to play, she could tell. She smiled. 'Yes—I'm excited!'

'Don't be, please.' He grinned. 'I couldn't stand the pressure.' He opened the door and she stepped outside into the mellow dusk. The scent of roses and oleander flowers drifted on the air as they went down the steps towards the waiting car. He put his guitar case on the back seat then opened the door for her. 'I was going to drive with the hood down, but I'll cover up if you think you'll be cold.'

'No, down's good.' She smiled. 'I'm a sucker for a convertible…'

'Me too—obviously!' He smiled and closed her door, strode round the car and slipped into the driver's seat. 'So, thanks again for looking after Alessia—and *huge* thanks for teaching her that song.' He shot her a mischievous smile as he started the engine. 'I now have the mother of all ear-worms playing in my head. There's every possibility that a few chords of the ant song might make it into my set tonight.'

She laughed. That song… All afternoon, memories had been trickling back, things her dad used to say escaping from her own lips as she'd walked with Alessia. It was still so strong inside her, the good stuff, that for a while she'd let go of her pain. *'You were thirteen'*—that was what Zach had murmured as he'd pulled her into his arms. At twenty-four, could she sift through those feelings again, find a grown-up perspective on things? She looked at Zach, his face shadowy in the twilight. It was unlikely that he'd bring up the subject of her family again in case it upset her, but she needed him to know that she *could* actually talk about her dad without turning into a snivelling mess.

'My dad taught me that song.' Zach threw her a glance and she gave him a little smile. 'We were camping one time and we found an ants' nest in the woods, just like Alessia and I did today. I was worried that the ants would come into the tent. I kept thinking I could feel them crawling on me, so my dad taught me the song…and I didn't mind the ants after that.' She could tell that he didn't know what to say. She took a deep breath. 'You know, they weren't even arguing… I had no idea they were planning to separate…so that morning, when Dad told me… I was—' She closed her eyes. 'You've no idea how angry I felt, with Dad especially, because he'd been my rock and I felt like he'd left me in the lurch… I'm sorry I wasn't able to talk to you about it the next day, especially after—'

'You've got nothing to be sorry for.' Zach drove through the gates then stopped the car. 'I understand everything. Your parents' split was a massive shock. On its own it would have been bad enough but facing down those kids at school—'

A deep, dark ache stirred inside her, spreading upwards until she could feel it at the base of her throat. She swallowed hard, whispered, 'Kids at school?'

He frowned. 'Yeah…isn't that at the heart of everything?'

She stared at him.

'The teasing… Sticking up for your parents' choices… Fighting their corner… Then having the rug pulled, just like that! It would make anyone angry.'

A car spun past, catching them in its headlights. Olivia looked down at her hands. How could it be that Zach had shone a light into shadows she didn't know existed? She felt his eyes on her, a little unravelling of something deep inside herself. She looked up, noticed the illuminated clock on the dashboard. 'We should go or you'll be late.'

He looked at her for a long second then threw the car into gear and pulled onto the road, accelerating hard. After a few moments he said, 'Are you okay?'

She stared ahead at the darkening valley, at the lights glinting from the houses scattered over the slopes. 'Yes—or at least I think I will be.'

* * *

'*Salve,* Zach!'

Smiling faces turned towards them as they stepped through the doorway. Olivia hung back. This was *his* night. She didn't want to saddle him with tedious introductions or with having to translate for her. In a corner there was a chair with a microphone stand set at guitar height. She threaded her way through the dark wooden tables and flickering tea lights until she found an empty seat close by, then she sat down and looked around.

It was an interesting interior, dark and intimate. In the past it might have been a wine cellar. The ceilings were arched, the walls were rough stone, illuminated at intervals with projector slides of music notes. *Cool!* She looked over to the bar, caught Zach's eye. He smiled at her, motioned to the beer bottles in his hand—one was for her—and carried on talking to a good-looking man in a pale linen jacket. The place was filling up fast. She figured that most of them were locals, the way they came in and sat down, the way they ordered without looking at the drinks list. She looked over at Zach again. He was talking to some other people now, trying to demonstrate some musical chord, struggling because of the beer bottles in his hand. He was animated, into it, she could tell. As she watched him, she couldn't stop her eyes travelling down… His jeans looked soft. They hung from his hips in just the right way. She should see the shape of his behind, wondered how it would feel to slip her hand into his back pocket.

Friend zone!

She shifted in her seat, slipped off her jacket, draped it over the back of her chair. When she looked over again he wasn't there and then she saw him making his way through the tables towards her, smiling.

'Sorry that took so long—I got caught.' He handed her a beer. 'I start in ten, so I'm going to go tune up. I've told Mario not to let your drink run dry.'

'Thanks, but I'm here for the music, not the drinks!'

He took a swig from his bottle. 'Now I'm nervous.'

'Why?'

He smiled, lowered his voice. 'Because I want you to like it.'

Those eyes…that smile… Impossible… 'I'm going to love it. Now, go on… Break a leg!'

She watched him walk away, watched him tuning his guitar, that same look of concentration on his face which she could see on Alessia's face sometimes. He was born to this, she could tell. Such fluidity in his shoulders and arms as he moved his hand along the fret, plucking strings, listening to the sound of the notes, little adjustments, listening again. He looked as if he was in another world; he looked at home there.

Someone behind the bar made an announcement she didn't understand, but there was a ripple of applause followed by a gradual hush. Zach caught her eye briefly, then bent his head and began to play.

She hadn't known what to expect, but from the first note he had her. Zach could *really* play. The agility of his fingers on the strings was hypnotising: fast, slow, teasing, spirited. And the way he cradled the guitar, moved his shoulder in and out as he played, it seemed as if he was physically connected to the melody. The combination of the music and the way he looked in his tee shirt and jeans, the way his hair touched his neck, the little contortions of his face as his fingers slid up and down the fret, took her breath away. She was unravelling, spiralling into a blissful kind of ache. More than anything she wanted to touch him, to feel his fingers on her skin, his body against hers. When he got to the end of his final piece and the bar filled with applause, she was a mess of hot tears and burning desire.

'Isn't he just brilliant?' A voice in her ear took her by surprise and she turned to see the good-looking man in the pale linen jacket, who'd been talking to Zach earlier. She hadn't noticed him sitting down beside her. He was clapping enthusiastically, smiling, leaning in so she could hear him above the noise. 'He is *so* talented. I love to hear him play.'

'That was my first time actually.' She pressed her fingers to her eyes and laughed, slightly embarrassed. 'I'm feeling a bit emotional…'

'Me too.' He smiled. 'I'm Milo, by the way. Milo Beneventi.'

'It's nice to meet you. I'm Olivia.' She smiled and sipped her beer, then she looked over at Zach. He was surrounded by friends and fans, but he must have sensed her somehow because suddenly he looked up, straight at her. He mouthed an invitation for her to go over, but she couldn't. She didn't trust herself not to throw her arms around him and press her lips to his. She needed to keep her distance, so instead she smiled at him then went to splash her face.

CHAPTER SIX

ZACH PUT HIS guitar case on the back seat, toyed with the key fob in his hand. He wondered what was going on with Olivia. She seemed quiet, preoccupied somehow. 'Do you want to go for a walk?'

She glanced at her watch. 'It's late.'

'That's a statement, not an answer.'

Her mouth quirked. 'I'll rephrase. Don't you think it's a little late for a walk?'

'No—not for me.' He ran a hand through his hair. 'Would you mind, Liv—please? It's just that I always feel restless afterwards…'

She held his gaze for a long moment then smiled. 'Okay. It's a lovely night.'

Yes! He pressed a button on the dash, watched the hood lifting up and over, then he locked the car. He threw her a smile. 'So… we'll begin our nocturnal wanderings in the very heart of Ravello. Are you ready?'

She lifted an eyebrow, looked as if she was stifling a giggle. 'I think so.'

He slid the key into his back pocket and led the way along a narrow street which opened into Piazza Centrale. The bars were closed, awnings pulled up, chairs and tables stacked. He spun round, walked backwards so he could see her face. 'This is the main square. It's heaving with tourists during the day. The cafés do a roaring trade.'

She turned a slow circle, looking at everything. 'That's a big church.'

'Duomo di Ravello! Strictly speaking, it's a cathedral.' He wondered if she'd say anything about his set. He'd felt her watching him while he was playing, had glanced up a couple of times, seen a depth of emotion in her eyes that had taken him by surprise, but she hadn't said anything yet and it seemed out of character somehow, especially when she'd been so excited about the gig. Maybe she was thinking about her parents again…or—he felt a knot tightening in his stomach—maybe she was thinking about Milo Beneventi.

After the show he'd been pulled into his usual crowd. He'd caught her eye, beckoned her over, but she'd held back. The next time he looked he'd seen her talking to Milo. Milo had fluent English so he supposed it made sense, but for some reason it bothered him, the way they seemed to be getting on so well. Suddenly, he'd wanted to be away from the crowds and the noise. He'd wanted to be with Olivia on her own, wanted to hear her thoughts about the music and about his playing, but ever since they left the bar she'd been quiet, a little distant, and he didn't understand why. Now he was wondering if she'd wanted to stay—because of Milo...

He watched her as she walked up the cathedral steps, noticed her slender calves in her white cropped jeans. He remembered the way she'd looked in the paddling pool, bare-legged, water drops glistening on her skin. He looked at his feet and swallowed hard. He couldn't let himself think about her like that, and he couldn't ask her what she thought about his playing either because that would seem needy. He sighed, followed her up the steps and turned to look across the square. The lights glowing from the houses on the opposite side of the valley looked like strings of fairy lights. He'd never noticed that before.

'I love those trees.' She was looking into the branches of the umbrella trees. Her hair was loose, falling at the side of her neck in gentle waves. When she pushed it away her perfume reached him on the air.

'They're called umbrella trees… Did you like my set?'

Damn!

She seemed to hesitate, then turned to look at him. 'Very much.' She smiled softly. 'You blew me away, Zach.'

He dropped his gaze, felt a tiny, powerful rush of joy. 'And you were going to mention this, when?'

Ouch!

'I mean, I'm glad you liked it—but you've been so quiet… I thought you might have been all over it—you know, giving me a full crit.' He flashed a smile. Perhaps he could claw back a shred of dignity by being light-hearted.

She started down the steps, then stopped to look back at him. 'You want a full crit?' Her smile was mischievous. 'Let's walk and I'll tell you my thoughts.'

'Okay.' He dived down the steps after her, then led her onto the Via del Episcopio. He felt like a cat on a hot tin roof. He had no idea why her opinion mattered so much, but it did.

'I don't know anything about music in a technical sense…' She threw him a little hopeless look. 'But honestly, I was mesmerised from the start, and that last piece you played…'

'Fauré's *Pavane*.'

'It made me cry.'

'I'm sorry—'

She nudged his shoulder playfully. 'Happy tears! I found it moving…haunting. Just lovely. Listening to you play, seeing the feeling you put into it and how good you are, I just kept wondering…'

'Wondering…?'

She stopped and gazed up at him. 'I just kept wondering why you're in the wedding business when you have such talent, such an obvious passion for music.'

As he held her gaze he remembered his father's words on the phone the day he'd broken the news that the band had split. *So you'll come home now…apply yourself to something more worthwhile?'*

He shrugged. 'Music's a tough business. I gave it my best shot, but I had to move on—I had to "come to my senses" as my father used to say.'

'Give up, you mean?'

'Whoa! I haven't given up! I still play.'

'Once a week—in a bar.'

'It's enough.'

'Is it?'

He stared at his feet. Somehow the conversation had taken a serious turn. He couldn't see why it mattered to her anyway. She was a swallow, passing through for the summer.

Why would she even care about his music and
what he did with it? When he looked up again
she was gazing at him, her eyes all softness
and warm light. A small breeze lifted her hair
and he couldn't help noticing her pale skin,
the swell of her breasts in the low V-neck she
was wearing.

She took a little step towards him. 'I'm sorry.
It's not my place, but you said you wanted a
full critique.' She seemed to be taking in every
detail of his face, reading every line and all the
lines in between. 'I think you have an amazing talent, Zach. I'm not qualified to know if
you're up to playing Carnegie Hall, but I can
see how much you love music and I think that's
why you feel restless after a gig… I think you
should do more with it, chase the thing you
love…'

Her words were making his head spin. He'd
buried his ambitions a long time ago and now
she was stirring the old dreams around, looking at him with such belief in her eyes and
something else too which was drawing him
like a magnet. He caught himself looking at
her mouth, the soft fullness of her lips, and he
felt himself drifting towards her, moving in
triple slow motion, losing himself in her eyes
and the shape of her mouth, the curve of her

cheek, and there was heat rising through his body, his hand reaching towards her face—

'Excuse me! Is this the way to Piazza Centrale?'

He snapped back to the moment, dropped his hand. An elderly man was looking at him. He took in the pale blue eyes, the checked shirt, the smiling grey-haired woman standing at the man's side. 'Er…yes! You're on the right road; just keep going down there and you'll come to it.'

'Thank you so much. Goodnight.'

As they strolled away, he became aware of his heart bumping against his ribs. What was happening to him? If the old couple hadn't interrupted him, he might have kissed Olivia. He probably, definitely would have kissed her, and then what? He felt a wash of relief. She'd taken him by surprise, caught him off-guard with her flattery, her enthusiasm for his playing and he'd felt young and free and he'd been about to…

Disaster!

He raked a hand through his hair and looked around. She'd walked a little distance away, seemed to be scrutinising something on the wall of a house. He wondered what she was thinking, hoped it wasn't going to be awkward between them now. She turned to look at him, smiled her usual warm smile.

'What does this say...? Something about André Gide and E M Forster—?'

He went over. 'It says they were guests here once.'

'Oh!' She walked on. 'Like me.'

Olivia poured herself a glass of water, added a chunk of lemon then went back to the computer. She studied the thumbnails on the screen. Saturday's bride had been beautiful. The groom had been handsome. Everything had looked perfect. And yet, as she scrolled through the pictures, she knew there was something missing. She'd had to work a bit harder with this couple, coaxing them into romantic poses. Perhaps they'd been camera shy, or perhaps they weren't naturally demonstrative, or perhaps it was just that they weren't really in love...

She lifted the glass to her lips and took a long sip, contemplated the gap between seeming and being... What *was* perfection anyway? She'd spent that day making perfect pictures of something that hadn't been perfect at all. She pushed her chair back and walked to the window. Her thoughts were tangling again...

She couldn't stop thinking about Zach and

that night in Ravello. The way his fingers had caressed the strings, the way he'd looked in his tee shirt and jeans… She'd tried to hold her feelings in, but without realising it she must have been sending out signals because he had definitely been going to kiss her. His eyes had gone all hazy and he'd been leaning in, stretching his hand towards her face, and her heart had been going nineteen to the dozen and she'd wanted it so badly, that kiss…and then the tourists had arrived.

Since that night she'd been telling herself that not kissing him had been for the best. She'd repeated all the usual mantras. He might be attracted to *her,* but he was still in love with his wife. He was her boss and there was Alessia, and this whole life he'd built here. Everything about Zach was complicated and *she* didn't want complications. She wanted a new beginning, a perfect man, a perfect wedding…to prove…what? A kaleidoscope of memories shattered into shifting circles—her dad, campfires and hiking, loading his belongings into the car, and the kids at school teasing and taunting. She squeezed her eyes shut. She couldn't think straight any more.

A knock on the door startled her and then she smiled when she remembered her last visitors—Alessia and Lucia—Lucia dressed to the nines, blushing about the 'thing' she was going to in town.

Boyfriend!

Maybe Lucia was bringing Alessia to say hello again—that would be nice—but when she opened the door, it wasn't Lucia.

'Zach!'

'Hi! I hope I'm not disturbing you...'

Jeans, white shirt, tiniest delicious waft of cologne.

'No! Come in. I'm only editing—'

'Good pictures?'

'No—they're rubbish.' He lifted an eyebrow and she laughed. 'Of course they're good. Can I get you something—a glass of lemon water?'

'No, I'm okay, thanks.'

She sat down on the sofa, hoping he couldn't tell that her heart was racing. 'So—?' She saw him noticing her legs in her denim cut-offs, golden-brown now instead of milky-white. He didn't sit down.

'I've just had a call from Milo Beneventi.'

He was studying her face as if he was looking for something, expecting a reaction. She didn't recognise the name. 'Okay...'

'From the bar—you were talking to him.'

'Erm...' Her mind was blank. The night at the bar, her head had been full of Zach and his playing. Music and longing. She could feel herself blushing, tingling at the memory…and then an image came to her: handsome face, pale linen jacket. He'd been sweet, could speak English. 'Ah—*that* Milo. Yes, I remember now.' She smiled but for some reason Zach didn't.

'He's an architect. Did he mention that?'

She tried to remember, drew another blank. 'No, I don't think so.'

'He's been involved with a property on Capri. It's nearing completion and he needs someone to take pictures. He wondered if you'd be interested.'

'Yes!' She parked her glass and stood up. 'I would be… Absolutely! I *love* architectural work, especially interiors. Before I started working for Ralph, I used to do bits and pieces for an arts magazine—galleries, places like that…'

She suddenly noticed the wariness in Zach's eyes and toned down her enthusiasm. Maybe he was worried she'd leave him in the lurch. He should know she would never do that; she'd committed herself to him for six weeks. She tried to warm him with a smile. 'What do *you* think? I mean… I'm here to work for you—I wouldn't want you to think—'

'I'm not thinking anything… It's absolutely fine, if you want to do it—'

'I do! It's a good opportunity! When I go back to London, I'm setting up on my own, shooting weddings, but I might have to be flexible at the beginning. A varied portfolio is currency. It'll help me to get other work while I'm building up my weddings.' She smiled. 'I'm grateful to you, Zach—you do know that?'

His eyes softened. 'I'll give you Milo's number. Have you got a pen?' Suddenly he broke into a smile and it was the old smile.

She laughed. 'I've heard that line somewhere before!' She picked up a pen and notepad from her desk and handed them over. 'Did he mention a timescale?'

Zach was mouthing the numbers as he wrote, little movements of his lips, the same lips that had come so close to kissing...

'As soon as possible, I think.' He placed the notepad and pen back into her hands.

'I'll need a decent tripod.'

'Michele will lend you one—he said if there was anything you needed—'

'I remember.'

'I'll speak to him, sort it out.' He took a step towards the door, then stopped. 'Milo said he'd pick you up in his boat—' She felt her eyes widening. This was getting better by the second. 'But I'll take you—'

'*You* have a boat?'

He nodded slowly. 'Yes. It's been laid up for a while.' His eyes were clouding over again. She wished she knew what he was thinking. 'I've been meaning to take it out for ages, but you know how it is—work gets in the way.' He seemed to drift for a moment, then he collected himself. 'Anyway, I'll take you.'

'Only if you've got time—I know how busy you are, Zach, and I don't want to put you to any trouble.'

'It's no trouble.' He shifted on his feet, fixed her with an even gaze. 'Like I said, the boat needs a run anyway.'

There was something bewitching about the light under the olive trees. The canopy was dense, the groundcover sparse. She thought that the trees must have gone feral a long time ago. She liked sitting here, wrapped in the mysterious blue-green light. She liked the emptiness, the silence that was barely threatened by the breeze whispering through the branches. It was a good place to think about things.

She lifted the camera to her eye, then put it down again. She wished she could see inside Zach's head. Ever since that night in Ravello he'd been acting differently. She'd done her utmost not to let the almost-kiss spoil their friendship, had tried to act as if nothing had happened, which it hadn't. Just like the other time nothing had happened.

So confusing.

The first time, he'd been holding her. She could see how physical proximity might have fuelled…but the second time they'd been standing on a narrow street, and she'd taken a step…and he'd taken a step…and she'd been feeling…but what about him? What did Zach feel? She sighed.

On the surface everything was normal, but she could tell he was preoccupied and it was bothering her. Perhaps he was reflecting on what she'd said about doing something with his music. Reaching back into the past, trying to pull old dreams into the present—that kind of thinking could fill your whole head, especially when you had a business to run, a daughter to think about… There would be other pressures too. Casa Isabella was a solid business—stepping away from it wouldn't go down well with his father, she supposed. Perhaps she should have kept her thoughts to herself, but watching him play, seeing the way he poured his heart into the music, realising how talented he was… It had moved her deeply and he *had* asked her what she thought. She'd had to tell him.

She wandered through the trees, little clouds of dust whirling around her feet. Parched earth, silence, mysterious light. She dropped to her knees, lifted the camera. Chinks of sunlight, bright rays piercing the gloom—light on dark—an interesting composition. She fired the shutter, listened to the sound of it reverberating.

She lowered the camera. At least the plans for her photoshoot on Capri had fallen into place. She'd made the arrangements with Milo, and Zach had secured the use of a tripod. He'd been seeing to his boat, getting it seaworthy, he said, but when he smiled at her there was no twinkle in his eyes. She'd tried to lighten his mood by offering to scrub the decks, but he'd said there was no need. He wasn't exactly shutting her out, but it felt as if he was stepping away. She remembered how she'd needed time to work through the stuff about her dad and it wasn't over yet—she was still trying to sort out her feelings. If Zach was preoccupied with his thoughts, there was nothing she could do except offer him a shoulder if he wanted it. He'd been there for her after all.

She got to her feet and brushed the dust off her knees. The next day he was taking her to Capri. Being alone with him on a boat might be the perfect opportunity for a heart-to-heart.

Zach checked the mooring rope then walked slowly down the jetty. He hadn't been onto the boat since Izzy died—hadn't been able to face it. They'd had such good times on *Django*—on their own, with family and with friends. Coming onto the boat again—checking things over—was something he'd needed to do for a long time. It had felt like his final frontier and it had drained him emotionally. The next day there'd be a new passenger, a new voyage to make.

His car was parked close by but he walked past it and onwards into the narrow streets of Minori. He needed a coffee, some time to think things through. Since that night in Ravello with Olivia, his emotions had been all over the place and he had to get a grip.

At a small café he took a seat outside and ordered an espresso. He gazed along the street, but it was Olivia's face he could see—her eyes… Twice, he'd come close to kissing her, which was confusing enough, but it wasn't only physical attraction he was feeling and that was confusing him even more. He liked that she was so fond of Alessia. He liked how much she'd been moved by his playing. He liked her warmth, her sense of humour, the way she was so easy to be with…

He sipped the strong bitter coffee, felt his mood darkening.

He wished he'd never told Milo what a great

photographer Olivia was, that night in the bar.
It had been hard enough watching them chatting together, but he'd never expected Milo to
suggest a photo shoot! This Capri caper was
his fault, and the whole thing was messing with
his head.

He felt the sun on his face and closed his
eyes.

Olivia!

He had no claim on her so whatever it was
that was churning him up about this trip, he'd
have to get it under control. Maybe it was a
protective thing…

That's it!

He'd taken his boat out of dry dock because
he wanted to make sure she'd be safe. It was
only natural, he told himself. She'd come to
Ravello to work for him after all, and there-
fore she was *his* responsibility. He pictured
Milo—that handsome face, that white smile,
that irrepressible charm. He opened his eyes
and reached for his cup. Milo seemed like a
nice guy, but at the end of the day he knew
nothing about him, and for that reason there
was no way on earth he was letting Olivia go
to Capri alone.

CHAPTER SEVEN

SHE WAS WEARING jeans and a white sleeveless shirt, sneakers and sunglasses. He couldn't detect any make-up, not that she needed any. Her hair was drawn into a ponytail, loose strands flying in the breeze. Her face was a picture—all smiles. He turned his gaze back to the sea, felt the power and thrust of the engine, the thrill of speeding through water. He'd missed this!

He looked at her again, felt a smile tugging at his lips. It was idiotic, he knew, to be analysing the nuances of her appearance, but the fact that she looked so…unadorned, pleased him. It meant she wasn't trying to attract Milo's attention, and for some reason that made him ridiculously happy. He leaned towards her, shouting over the engine noise. 'What do you think?'

'Fantastic!' she yelled back. 'I don't want it to end!'

'Want to drive?'

She widened her eyes, excited. 'Can I?'

'Sure!' He slowed right down and slipped out of the helmsman's seat.

She glanced at him, then gingerly took his place and put her hands on the wheel.

'What do I do?'

Her face and arms looked tanned against her white shirt. He noticed a sprinkle of tiny freckles on her nose, caught the scent of her perfume as he stepped in again to steady the wheel.

'It's easy.' He pointed to a distant buoy bobbing on the water. 'See the marker up there?'

She turned to look at him, her face so close that he couldn't stop himself glancing at her mouth, that soft little pout, the briefest dart of her tongue as she concentrated on what he was saying.

'Just aim for that, keeping left.' He smiled. 'Ready?'

'I guess!'

He dropped the throttle and she gave a little shriek as the boat ploughed forward. She was sitting bolt upright, eyes fixed on the buoy, arms flexing as she handled the wheel. It was hard not to laugh. 'You're a natural!'

She grinned, not taking her eyes off the water. 'You think so?'

'Oh, yes!' Suddenly, he had an idea, leaned in. 'Will you be okay for a moment?'

Head rigidly pointing forward. 'Don't leave me...'

'I'm not leaving you... I'm just going onto the foredeck.'

'Why?'

He laughed. 'Never mind why—just keep steering!' He moved away, found a position on the bows and took out his phone.

When she saw what he was doing she started to laugh, yelling, 'No! Don't you dare!'

'Keep your eyes on the road!'

She looked so great, so happy steering the boat, that he had to take a picture...and he could tell she didn't really mind. She started pulling faces, striking poses—looking for land, doing Jack Sparrow—then she took her hands off the wheel and stretched out her arms—*Titanic*!

He was laughing so hard that he only noticed the buoy when they were twenty metres away. 'Olivia! Go left!'

He leapt to the helm, throttled back then seized the wheel, steering clear of the marker with metres to spare.

'Did we nearly hit—?'

'No! Yes! Possibly—but it wasn't your fault.'

He grinned. 'I was distracting you and, to be fair, I told you to aim for the marker!'

She grimaced. 'I almost crashed.'

'Just like *Titanic*!' He laughed and nudged her shoulder. 'Forget about it.' He dropped the throttle and the boat took off again. As the wind whipped at her hair he saw her cheeks lifting into a smile. He leaned in. 'Want to go faster?'

Wide eyes. 'It goes faster?'

He put his hand on the throttle, smiling. 'Hold on!' He pushed the lever and the boat surged forward, ripped across the water, bouncing hard then flying, bouncing, flying— and she was squealing with laughter, gripping the rail so tightly that he couldn't help laughing too. It was the best he'd felt for days…this joy of being on the water, the speed, the sunshine, her laughter… It felt like freedom.

He followed the coast so she could see the towns—pastel houses crammed onto impossible slopes—then he turned west. As they approached Capri, he slowed down. Milo was meeting them at the property, a secluded place with a private mooring on the eastern side of the island. Olivia had pushed her sunglasses onto her head and was gazing at the craggy slopes of bleached rock, marvelling at the tufts of trees and shrubs which grew on the inhospitable cliffs.

She caught his eye. 'Don't you find this amazing?'

'Every time!' He took off his sunglasses and slipped them into his shirt pocket. 'There are some underground caves on Capri that you really should see. You'd love the light! Emerald, turquoise. It's stunning.'

She turned, studied his face for a moment then shot him a little smile. 'You seem happier today…'

'Happier?'

She nodded. 'You've seemed preoccupied recently. I've been worrying that it's got something to do with what I said…about your music. I didn't mean to upset—'

'You didn't upset me.' He looked along the shoreline, trying to spot the mooring. 'You were very enthusiastic. I was pleased that you enjoyed my playing, flattered that you think I could do something with it…'

She was still looking at him, a little frown on her face. 'So—if it's not anything I said, what is it then—what's wrong?' She nudged his shoulder. 'I mean, fair's fair! I cried all over *your* shirt—the least I can do is listen if you want to talk…' She tucked some loose strands back into her ponytail and smiled, eyes wide and gentle, drawing him in again. He looked away, scouring the shoreline. Perhaps the mooring was on the other side of the outcrop. Her eyes on him, searching his face, wanting an answer. He couldn't tell her that he was a ball of confusion and that she was rolled up in it. Maybe he could tell her about the boat, about the sadness it had stirred up inside him. If he told her, maybe she'd be satisfied and wouldn't dig any deeper. He dropped the throttle a little more so that the boat was barely moving.

'It's the boat.'

Her forehead creased. 'The boat?'

He nodded. 'I haven't been on it since Izzy died. We both loved this boat, had great fun with it, but after she passed I couldn't bring myself to… Besides, I had other priorities. Getting *Django* out of dry dock has been hard—'

Her face fell. 'I feel bad now—for putting you through that. Milo could have picked me up—'

'No!' He checked himself. 'What I mean is, I couldn't let him do that when I have a perfectly good boat. I *wanted* to get it back out on the water, and you needing a ride was just the push I needed. I knew I'd have to face it some time and now I have, thanks to you!' He smiled. 'If I look happy it's because I am.'

'So you're okay, really?'

'Yes! Really!' The throaty burble of the engine, the sloshing of waves against the hull filled a long, silent moment. She looked as if she was about to say something but suddenly, up ahead, he caught sight of Milo's boat moored at the end of a long jetty, the man himself waving.

'Wow, Milo! This place is amazing.'

'You like it? That's good. If you like it, it will make your photographs *splendide*.'

Olivia couldn't help liking Milo. His accent was charming, *he* was charming. Warm brown eyes, thick dark hair. He was tall, his body well-honed under his expensive shirt and designer jeans.

As he showed them around, he explained that the property had been designed as a deluxe holiday let for couples. 'So... I started with a traditional structure then incorporated modern elements, like steel for the canopy and lots of glass—to make the most of the view.'

Zach ran his hand down a steel column. 'I like this—it's unexpected.'

Milo smiled. 'Thank you, Zach. Architects enjoy playing with expectation.'

The interior was modern and minimalist—

pale marble floors, white walls. There was a magnificent master bedroom with luxury en-suite bathroom, a sleek white kitchen with brushed steel appliances and slate worktops. The spacious sitting room, furnished with white leather sofas and a black marble coffee table, opened to an al fresco dining area which overlooked the sea.

'It's romantic—' Olivia conjured an image of Zach walking across the room towards her—faded jeans, shirt unbuttoned one notch lower than decent, those eyes. 'But it's also got a calm, timeless vibe, like a sanctuary.'

'Exactly!' Milo smiled. White teeth. 'Calm, romantic, secluded—that's what the client wanted, so if that's what you are feeling then I have succeeded!' He had such a sunny smile… delightful.

She spun around slowly, assessing the ambient light, thinking about shooting angles, when she caught Zach staring at her. He looked preoccupied again. She wondered if he was thinking about the boat, memories of Isabella…

Milo was extracting a silver ice bucket from a length of bubble wrap. 'So, we'll begin shooting outside while we have the morning light, then we'll come inside, okay?'

'Sounds good to me.' She knelt to open her camera bag, taking out the things she needed.

When she looked up, Zach was leaning against the wall, examining a painting.

Zach!

This shoot was going to be so dull for him. She glanced outside. Milo was polishing two glasses with a cloth, carefully arranging them on the table next to the ice bucket. She stood up, kept her voice low. 'Listen, Zach…you're going to get so bored. Seriously! Watching this kind of shoot is like watching paint dry. You don't have to stay. I'll be fine with Milo, really!'

He came towards her. 'I don't mind staying.' He looked at her evenly then shifted his gaze to the man outside. 'I mean, how long will it take?'

Why was he so distracted? She cleared her throat to get his attention. 'Two or three angles per room, exteriors from all sides, I guess, maybe some shots of the view—' She gave a little shrug. 'A couple of hours, probably.'

'You don't want me to help with anything?' He turned to look at Milo again, and Olivia followed his gaze. Milo had moved on to wiping the chair backs with a cloth, his movements deft, his face tense with concentration.

She couldn't help smiling. 'I think Milo's got it covered.'

'Okay.' Zach's smile didn't reach his eyes. He slipped his sunglasses from his shirt pocket and put them on. 'If you think you'll be okay, then I'll take the boat for a blast.'

She pulled a cross-eyed face. 'I'm only trying to save your sanity.'

'It's probably too late for that.' He smiled softly. 'You've got my number, yeah, just in case?'

She nodded. 'Are you *worried* about me?'

He seemed to falter. 'No—not worried. I'll see you in a while.' He turned away, walked towards the terrace.

'Have fun!'

He threw up his hand in a backward wave.

She watched him pause to speak to Milo, and then he was striding towards the cliff steps. Moments later he was gone.

Distractedly, she opened up the tripod and attached the camera. Zach had been through a great sadness in his life but he was sociable, likeable, an easy-going person. Yet, minutes after they'd arrived, he'd become withdrawn. Something was eating him up and she couldn't figure it out. She looked up, saw Milo beckoning from the terrace. She waved back and picked up the tripod. She'd have to forget about Zach for a while. She needed to concentrate on the shoot.

* * *

Milo was easy to work with. He positioned things without her having to ask, styled the shots with an expert eye. The props he'd brought were tasteful: cashmere throws, pillar candles, crystal glasses. As they worked, he chatted about architecture, art and music...

'Zach is very talented with the guitar...' He smoothed a throw across the bed, turning back an edge to show the fringe. 'Sometimes when he plays, I feel a sadness in his heart...' He stood back. 'How's that—do you need me to pull it back a little more?'

She looked through the viewfinder. 'No! That's perfect.' She took three shots, different exposures. She thought about the boat, the sadness Zach had talked about just hours ago. 'I suppose, on some level, playing gives him an outlet...' She detached the camera from the tripod, gave it to Milo so he could check the last few shots.

'Olivia, these are perfect! It's a wrap!' He flashed his white smile. 'We're a good team! How about a glass of wine?'

It was a relief that Milo was pleased with her work. She smiled. 'A glass of wine sounds like a very good idea.'

He handed her the camera. 'Can I help you pack up?'

'No, thanks.' She gave him a little shrug. 'I count it out and count it in again—force of habit, so I know I've got everything.'

'Okay. *I* will go and open the wine!' He left the room and she smiled to herself. The wine he'd brought as a prop had been chilling in an ice bucket on the dining table for over an hour. It would be perfect by now, and didn't she deserve a little celebration? Her first overseas commercial shoot! Milo was happy, and *she* had more classy photos for her portfolio. She folded the tripod and packed away her kit. When she went through to the sitting room Milo handed her a glass, then raised his own.

'Thank you, Olivia, for a successful shoot. Here's to many more in the future!'

She touched her glass to his and took a long sip. It would be great to shoot more Italian interiors. Milo would be a good contact. She suddenly realised he was watching her, a smile in his eyes.

'You like?'

'Mmm—it's delicious.'

He looked pleased. He motioned to the sofa. 'Let's take the weight off. Is that what you say?'

'Yes! Your English is very good.' She dropped onto the long sofa, ran her hand over the leather. It felt soft, yielding. Expensive.

Milo sat on the sofa too, a little distance away. He took a sip from his glass, crossed one leg over the other.

'So, forgive me, but what did you mean by *an outlet* when you were talking about Zach's playing?'

'I meant that maybe playing gives him a way of expressing his grief…'

'Grief?' Milo frowned. 'What grief?'

'I…thought you knew…about his wife… She died.'

Milo's face blanched. 'I had no idea…' He shook his head a little. 'I don't know Zach very well… I only moved here a year ago. What happened to his wife?'

'I don't know. I haven't wanted to ask—but I do know she passed a couple of years ago.'

'Oh, dear.' To her surprise, Milo's eyes began to fill with tears. 'This sad news is setting me off…'

She leaned forward. 'Are you all right?'

He put his glass down, wiped his eyes with his hands. 'I'm sorry; forgive me. I get emotional because I lost someone too—it's why I came to Capri. I couldn't stay in Naples after Sergio died…'

Sergio!

'He had a cancer of the pancreas… We found out too late.' He sniffed, took a drink from his glass. 'I keep myself to myself most of the time, so no one knows. I don't socialise much…but I like the bar, listening to the music. It's nice.'

She thought of Zach on the boat that morning—*'If I look happy it's because I am.'* Was that the truth or had he been trying to make her feel better about the boat? Was he still trapped in his grief like poor Milo? That night in Ravello, when he'd reached out to her, that look in his eyes. The threads inside her head were tangling again.

She took a small sip of wine then set down the glass. 'I suppose it must be hard to move on when you've lost the love of your life…'

Milo's eyes filled with fresh tears. 'It's not hard, Olivia. It's im-pos-sible.' He began to sob and for a moment she felt completely helpless, then she did the only thing she could think of. She moved along the sofa and wrapped her arms around him.

Zach began to untie *Django* from her mooring then stopped and re-tied the rope. He couldn't leave. He'd brought Olivia to Capri so he could keep an eye on her—on Milo. Jetting off around the island would defeat the object. He sighed, scaled the short ladder and jumped aboard. He yanked a bottle of water from the fridge near the helm, took it onto the foredeck and sank onto one of the sun pads.

When they'd set out this morning he'd felt great. He'd worked through his sadness about getting the boat out, had loved every minute of their little voyage to Capri. And Olivia had loved it too—the views, the speed, the feeling of flying across the water. Her face had been a picture, glowing, full of life.

Alive!

It had been a long time since he'd felt like that. But then somehow, up there, looking around the property, he'd started noticing little looks between Olivia and Milo.

Noticing or imagining?

He swallowed hard. And then she'd said he could go, that she'd be fine with Milo. He snapped the cap off the bottle, swigged down an icy mouthful of water. Had she really been trying to save his sanity or was there another reason she'd wanted him to leave? He looked up at the house on the cliff, and suddenly an image came to him—Olivia in Milo's arms. As his stomach churned, he suddenly realised that he was sick with jealousy.

He dropped his head into his hands and groaned. He liked Olivia—liked her so much that the thought of her being with anyone else was driving him crazy. He hadn't realised until

this moment how far gone he already was…
She was doing something to him, making him
think about things that were too difficult to
think about…like caring for someone again.
But he was stuck. How could he think about
moving on when he'd hadn't said goodbye to
Izzy? Her face that night, laughing… *'I'm
fine, Zach. Stop worrying.'* The aftershock,
the dazed limbo and always Alessia's tragic
eyes, looking for her *mamma*, crying for a loss
she couldn't articulate. He'd fallen on the renovation of Casa Isabella like a half-starved ani-
mal, worrying at it like a dog with a bone. He
never thought he'd step back, begin to see a
wider view. But it *was* happening. Olivia was
making it happen, and she had no idea what
she was doing to him. Instead, she was in the
house on the cliff with Milo Beneventi.

He pressed the cold bottle to his forehead.
He was scared to look back, scared to look
forward. He didn't know what to do… All he
knew was that he had two hours to talk himself off the ledge.

'Zach!'

It took him a split-second to take in the open
wine bottle, the two empty glasses, her hands
wrapped around Milo's. Her eyes. Milo's eyes.
His gut twisted tight. Just minutes ago, on the

boat, he'd reminded himself that Olivia was a free agent, but he hadn't expected to walk in on something like this.

Breathe.

'Hi! How did it go?'

Smile.

She was standing up, smiling. 'Really well.'

Milo was standing up, smiling. 'Olivia is a joy to work with!'

The pair of them, smiling at each other, exchanging little looks. It was an effort to control his voice. 'That's great! I'm glad it went well.'

Milo motioned to the wine bottle. 'Would you like a drink, Zach?'

He couldn't imagine anything worse. All he wanted to do was escape. He spied Olivia's bag and tripod in the corner.

'I'm sorry, Milo, but we have to get going.' He gave a little shrug. 'Something came up.' He turned to Olivia. 'Are you good to go?'

'Yes.' He could tell she was trying to read his thoughts. 'The gear's all packed.'

He went for her bag and tripod. When he looked up, she was giving Milo a hug.

'I'll send the photos as soon as I can.' She stepped back, looked deeply into Milo's eyes 'You take care now. I'll see you soon.'

Zach realised he was grinding his teeth.

'Liv, I'm sorry, but we really *do* have to go.' He leaned forward, shook Milo's hand. 'Sorry, Milo. I'll see you around some time…'

He started walking towards the terrace, heard Olivia's quick footsteps behind him. He didn't look back but hurried down the steep winding steps which led to the jetty. He stood aside to let her onto the boat first, then handed her the tripod.

As she took it from him, her eyes locked on his. 'What's happened?'

He fought back a wave of guilt for dragging her away on false pretences. 'Nothing's happened.'

'You said, *"Something came up"*—what came up? Is everyone all right—Alessia?'

Her sweet concern for his family increased his misery. He picked up the camera bag, handed it up to her. 'Everyone's fine.' He attempted a reassuring smile, then untied the boat, threw the rope on deck and jumped aboard.

'So, what's up then?'

I think I might be falling for you.

He broke away from her gaze, took the wheel and turned the key in the ignition. The engine kicked and slowly he backed *Django* away from the jetty.

She came to sit beside him at the helm.

'What's going on, Zach? I feel like you're mad at me and I don't understand…'

He throttled forward slowly, pointing the boat towards the open sea. When he turned to look at her, he hated the bewilderment he could see in her eyes, hated himself for being the cause of it. He sighed. 'I could never be mad at you, Liv. I just need to get back, that's all. I… I've got a meeting.'

'Oh! I didn't know.' She dropped her sunglasses over her eyes. 'You didn't mention it before.'

She was staring into the distance, her lips pressed together, a small frown creasing her forehead. He wished he could tell her what he was feeling, but he was a mess and he knew that whatever he said would come out all wrong. He pushed the lever, felt the boat lifting in the water, but this time she didn't laugh and squeal.

The wind tugged at his hair, the growl of the engine filled his ears and in his head, over and over again, he replayed the scene he'd just witnessed. He'd walked in on something. They hadn't tried to hide it… Their hands had remained clasped, their affection obvious. He felt his jaw tighten as he tried to bury his anguish. Olivia was single and he had no right to feel put out if she liked Milo. He glanced at her, noticed goosebumps on her bare arms. He rummaged under his seat for his old hoodie and handed it to her, raising his voice over the engine noise. 'You're cold—take this!'

She gave him a little smile, eyes hidden by her shades. 'Thanks!' She pulled it on, wrapped it tightly around herself. Out of the corner of his eye, he saw her drawing the hood against her cheek, breathing in the scent of the fabric, and for some reason the small action seemed to ground him.

He thought about the night in the bar, what he'd seen in her eyes as he was playing, the way she'd looked at him on that narrow street in Ravello. It felt wrong that she could like Milo. How could she like Milo when, from the very first moment she'd looked at him, he'd felt something between them?

How could she like Milo?

Suddenly she was pushing her sunglasses up, leaning in so he could hear her voice. 'Zach! How much do you know about Milo?'

Was she tapping him for information? A fresh wave of misery crashed over him and he swallowed hard. 'Virtually nothing.'

She stood up and pressed her back against the windscreen so she was facing him. The breeze was buffeting her hair, loosening it from her ponytail, but she didn't seem to notice. She looked at him squarely, raised her voice above the engine. 'So…you don't know that he moved to Capri after his partner, Sergio, died?'

It took a moment for her words to sink in. 'Sergio?'

She nodded, shouted, 'Sergio was the love of his life! Had pancreatic cancer… They found it too late.'

In his head, images scrolled in slow motion. Milo's eyes filled with—sadness! Deep looks… Clasped hands… Liv stroking Milo's shoulder as she was saying goodbye. He could see it all so clearly now. She'd been comforting Milo, not… He groaned inwardly—he'd been such a fool, blinded by jealousy, and she'd worked it out, seen right through him. She was gazing at him, hair blowing all around her face, and he could hear all the words she wasn't saying.

He shook his head, spoke half to himself. 'I've been an idiot…'

'What?' She was frowning. 'Can we please stop the boat? I can't hear you!'

He throttled down, switched off the engine. The boat reared and fell back into the dark shifting water, rolling and pitching, little sloshing sounds framing the fresh silence.

He dropped his hands from the wheel, moistened his lips.

'I've been an idiot... I thought—'

'I know.'

She was looking at him, reading him like a book, he felt, but he didn't mind. It was a relief to be found out. He smiled, gave a little shrug. 'I suppose I've blown my cover...'

Her eyebrow lifted, warm light playing across her irises. 'Probably.'

He took a step towards her, wished he could stop his heart banging against his ribcage. 'I like you, Liv.' Another step forward. 'I didn't realise how much until today...'

Her eyes were holding his, hair softly blowing across her cheek.

'So...?' Her voice sounded husky.

He reached a hand to her face, felt her melting into his touch, and then slowly he lowered his mouth to hers. Warmth...softness... the taste of wine on her lips... For a moment he lingered there, letting the sensation wash over him, and then he was pulling her closer, desire catching him like a wildfire, torching every nerve in his body.

He pulled her hard against him and she sighed, slid her hands over his shoulders and up into his hair. Her lips were parting and he was taking everything, kissing her deeply, losing himself in her. It had been so long since he'd had this—felt this—he couldn't stop. He worked his hands under the hoodie, under her blouse, senses swimming as his fingers connected with the warm smoothness of her back. He could feel her hands sliding into the back pockets of his jeans, drawing him closer, and it was almost too much. It occurred to him that he could anchor the boat, take her down into the cabin—but was he ready? She was here to work for him…and there were things he needed to get straight in his head. He liked her so much, wanted her so much, but he had to slow down, take a moment.

He took her face in his hands and broke off breathlessly. Her eyes were hazy, her cheeks flushed, lips swollen. He steadied himself, pressed his forehead to hers. 'Wait—'

'Wait?'

'Just for a moment…'

He felt her arms sliding around his waist, the softness of her hair on his neck as she laid her head against him. He wrapped his arms around her, buried his lips in her hair. 'I'm sorry.'

'You don't have to be sorry.' She pulled her head away from his chest, looked into his face. 'It must be hard…after losing…' She pressed her lips together. 'Milo says it's impossible for him to move on…'

He studied her face, seeing little glimmers of light in her eyes. What was he seeing there? Fear? Longing? Something else…?

He sighed. 'I don't think it's impossible… It's just that everything feels so new…like uncharted waters.' He smiled. 'Maybe I need to stay in the shallows for a while. Can you understand that?'

She touched his cheek, smiled. 'The shallows are warm and safe. They're a good place to start.'

CHAPTER EIGHT

OLIVIA WATCHED ZACH and Alessia romping around in the water. Minori beach was a world away from the sands of West Wittering and those shivery mornings with her dad. *'Come on, Liv. It's bracing.'* That cold slab of wet sand under her feet which made her arches ache, that breathless tiptoe advance, the icy creep of water up her legs, her dad laughing. He used to pull her in. The breath would freeze in her lungs as the waves closed over her shoulders. She'd come up kicking and gasping, then laughing because it wasn't so bad after all. *'You've got to dive right in.'* That was what he used to say.

She drew her legs up and hugged her knees. Over the past couple of weeks she'd found herself thinking about her dad quite a bit, teasing out all the little knots in her head. Since the day he left, she'd been blaming him for everything. But Zach had been right. The real feeling of betrayal had sprung from the years she'd spent rebuffing jokes about her family from the kids at school. She'd felt so small and stupid when it came out that her dad had left. Not that they'd joked about that exactly, but she'd seen it in their eyes, she'd felt the warm breath of their whispers. That was when her self-confidence had evaporated and that was when the fantasy had started. Her fixation with finding a perfect man, a man whose heart belonged only to her. A man who wasn't afraid to commit. A man who wanted to marry her.

Zach had Alessia on his shoulders now, holding her hands, scuffing through the little waves. Olivia couldn't help smiling as she watched them. Since arriving in Italy, her narrow view of perfection seemed to have expanded. Being with Zach was helping her to see things differently. That day on the boat, when he'd kissed her for the first time, she'd been filled with dismay when he pulled away. She'd thought he was changing his mind. She'd given him a get-out, told him what Milo had said about moving on, but he'd taken her by surprise with his answer and then he'd said, *'Everything feels so new...like uncharted waters...'* She'd never looked at things that way before. She'd focused so much on what he'd had with Isabella that she'd never thought that there could be anything new for him to discover. His words had bolstered her spirits that day.

'Hey!' He lifted Alessia off his shoulders and dropped to his knees on the sand. 'Why didn't you come in?'

Blue eyes, still giving her butterflies. She reached a towel out of the bag and wrapped it around Alessia tightly. 'What have I got here? A bug in a rug?' Alessia giggled, shrugged out of the towel and plonked her bottom onto the sand. She picked up a little spade, started to fill a yellow plastic bucket.

Zach was rubbing his shoulders with a towel, smooth golden skin, biceps flexing as he worked the towel over his body. She released a slow breath. How could she tell him she was getting tired of life in the shallows?

She smiled. 'I was happy watching.' He had just the right amount of dark hair, well defined abs, the dusky trail leading... 'Besides, it's nice for you two to be together on your own.'

He laid his towel on the sand. 'It was lovely in the water, wasn't it, Alessia?'

Alessia looked up, quirked her mouth. 'It was *as-ton-ish-ing.*'

Olivia laughed. 'I'm never going to live that down, am I?'

He stretched out beside her. She felt his hand

on her bare back, his fingers moving slowly up and down. Her stomach clenched. Did he have any idea what he was doing to her? She felt his lips on her shoulder. 'What about dinner tonight?'

She turned to look at him. 'You mean, *going out* for dinner?'

He nodded, fixed her with a darkening gaze. 'Somewhere nice…'

She smiled. 'Somewhere nice sounds…very nice!'

His lips grazed her shoulder again. 'I'll pick you up at seven.'

She could feel his fingers at the base of her back tracing warm circles round and round and, as she held his gaze, she could see a steady heat building. She swallowed hard, forced out an even breath. 'I'm looking forward to it.'

'Zach, this is beautiful!'

Happy light in her smile, eyes sparkling. It's what he'd been hoping for. He tugged her close, kissed her hair, breathed in the soft musk of her perfume. The warmth of her body flowed into the hand he'd pressed to her waist and he could feel it moving through his veins, transforming itself into the stirrings of an immeasurable want. He released her quickly, stepped back so she could follow the waiter who was leading them across the terrace to a balcony table overlooking the sea and the tangerine heat of the sunset.

He'd never been to Ambruosi, the restaurant at the Palazzo Broccardi. That was part of its appeal—he'd wanted to take her somewhere that would be new for both of them. More than anything, he wanted some time alone with her, away from work, away from anything familiar, and this was perfect! A sunset, a balmy evening, candles on the table and Piazzolla's *Oblivion* playing in the background. He ordered wine, watched as Olivia looked around delightedly. Such a lovely face, little gold studs glinting in her earlobes, her neck smooth and lightly tanned.

Two weeks had passed since the shoot on Capri. Two more weddings had taken place at Casa Isabella plus a last-minute renewal of vows celebration that had disrupted their routine. Both he and Olivia had been busy. He'd managed to spend some time with Alessia, and Olivia had accompanied him to his gigs at the bar but, apart from evening walks in the garden and the occasional sundowner on the terrace, they hadn't seen much of each other.

In truth, he'd been preoccupied with business matters. His father had floated the idea of a second wedding venue in Italy, wanted

Zach to start searching for a suitable property. For some reason it had felt as if the walls were closing in.

He'd needed their afternoon at the beach… time with Alessia and Olivia, living in the moment. The memory of Liv in her swimsuit, smooth skin on her arms and legs, the way her back had felt, warm and silky… He hadn't wanted to stop his fingers moving over her skin, and now she was sitting here in a soft dress that skimmed in all the right places, her face glowing. It was hard to keep focus.

When the waiter had poured the wine he lifted his glass. 'Here's to freedom!'

'Freedom?'

'Getting away from the grind…'

She lifted an eyebrow. 'I'll drink to that.' She took a sip from her glass and set it down. 'It's relentless, isn't it…running a wedding venue. I thought wedding photography was demanding but at least it's just one day—' She pulled a thinking face. 'Followed by three days on the computer, admittedly, but the venue thing, dealing with people all the time—that's full-on.'

He took a long sip of his wine, held it in his mouth for a moment. *'It's relentless.'* She was reading his mind! He pictured his father at the other end of the phone. *'Casa Isabella's been a huge success. We should repeat the winning formula with a new venue.'* He pushed the thought away—dwelling on it would only make him morose.

She toyed with the stem of her glass. 'Zach, why don't you employ a manager?'

His heart caught. A tiny needle-prick. He picked up his glass again. She was looking at him, eyes keen, endlessly curious. That feeling again, walls closing in. He sipped his wine then drew a measured breath.

'I suppose it's got a lot to do with Izzy…the fact that she loved it so much. I've felt a responsibility for…' His eyes drifted to the sun, fading to a blush on the horizon. Unpacking the past. Maybe he should talk about things more. Open up. He turned back to Olivia, met her gaze.

'Izzy's family had a restaurant in Naples. She grew up with it, helped out, but she was ambitious. She had big plans! She studied hospitality and business at university. After she got her degree, she found an investor, persuaded her family to renovate the restaurant, take it more upmarket. That's where I met her.' He smiled. 'I'd been bumming around Europe in a band, playing little gigs, deluding myself that we were going places. We got to Naples and our singer bailed, then the band split and

I was killing time, wondering what to do… I went into Izzy's restaurant one night and she took my order… I went back the next day, and the day after that…' He leaned back in his chair. 'I suppose we had a lot in common, my family being in the hotel business…

'I wanted to stay in Naples but I needed a career change, needed to make some money, so I went home, started working for Merrill Hotels. Dad was thrilled—his son and heir was finally on the right track. I started a new line of boutique hotels, high-end places. It was going well but I wanted to marry Izzy and live in Italy, so I decided to buy a hotel here. Dad liked the idea of a European expansion, said he'd invest. So I moved to Italy and started looking, but then Izzy's father died and Lucia didn't want to carry on with their restaurant any more. Izzy and I were married by that time. It seemed like the perfect moment for us to find a hotel we could run together…

'We did a road trip, viewed a lot of places that didn't quite hit the mark, and then Izzy found Casa Dorato—that's what it was called then—it means "Golden House".' His mouth suddenly felt dry and he picked up his glass, took a slow slip. 'It wasn't the going concern we'd been looking for. It was in a terrible state but we saw something in it and Izzy said we should turn it into the most romantic wedding venue on the Amalfi Coast.' He smiled. 'My father took some persuading because of the renovation cost but Izzy could be very persuasive…'

'And then you lost her…' Olivia's eyes were glistening.

He swallowed hard. 'Aside from the grief, I felt…stranded. Does that make sense?' It suddenly occurred to him that Olivia, of all people, would understand. 'Like when your dad left—that feeling of the rug being snatched from under your feet. I had a half-renovated *palazzo* and a baby. The only thing I could think of was finishing what we'd started. Knowing how much Izzy had wanted it was reason enough for me to do it…and then, when it was finished, I wanted to make sure it was a success—for her.'

He smiled. 'I know I *should* get a manager. For one thing, I need to spend more time with Alessia but letting go isn't all that easy.'

'Maybe it's because you still feel stranded—' Olivia was gazing at him over the rim of her wine glass. 'I mean, if you let go of the reins, what comes next? It's a scary thought.' She sipped her wine. 'I think it's why I stayed with Ralph for so long. The alternative seemed so much worse—striking out on my own again—

maybe failing again. In the end he forced my hand. Did I ever tell you that?'

'No! You said you were going out on your own.'

She laughed. 'Well, the truth is that Ralph gave me a little push, and then you called and offered me this great opportunity—I mean, what are the chances?' She smiled. 'Maybe that's all *you* need—a little push.'

As the waiter set out their entrées he turned her words over in his head. Letting go...*what comes next?*...chances... Could Olivia be his second chance? Maybe it was time to come out of the shallows...

Zach reached for her hand. 'Dance with me...'

They were walking along a tree-lined path that ran below the restaurant terrace. Small footlights illuminated the tree trunks, fairy lights twinkled in the branches. She recognised the music drifting down from the restaurant, eddying around them like little waves. She smiled hesitantly. 'Here?'

'Why not...? There's music!'

There was something in his eyes that told her resistance would be futile, so she smiled and stepped into his arms. He pulled her close, started to move her around in a slow circle. His hand at her back felt firm and warm.

She looked into his face. 'I know this music…'

'It's famous! *Gymnopédies* by Eric Satie. I play it sometimes…' His eyes went hazy and he leaned in, brushed her lips with his, then he straightened and spun her around quickly, as if she wasn't already dizzy enough. 'Satie was very eccentric. He only ate white food, and he had a whole wardrobe of identical suits so he didn't waste time choosing what to wear.'

She smiled. 'You know so much!'

His eyes locked on hers. 'When you have an interest, you tend to absorb details…'

'Mmm…' She was thinking about the beach, details like the curve of his shoulder as he'd dried himself, the defined abs, the trail of dark hair leading… He chose that moment to pull her closer, pelvis to pelvis. She swallowed a little gasp and closed her eyes. Thighs, hips, torso—moving against her—steady heat flowing from his body into hers. She could feel desire guiding his every move and it was what she'd been waiting for—wasn't it?

His hair skimmed her cheek as his lips touched her neck. She melted into his warmth, the sensation of his mouth on her skin. She couldn't fight this—she didn't want to fight it. She tangled her fingers into his hair, tipped her head back as his lips grazed the skin at the base of her throat, and it was like falling…letting go… but could she really let go without knowing what was going on in his head?

'Zach, please stop…'

He pulled away, eyes burning into hers. 'Stop?'

Her ribs felt tight. She couldn't pinpoint the exact moment she'd fallen in love with him, but ever since that moment her lines had blurred. She wanted this…wanted him, but she needed a moment to think… If he was coming out of the shallows it had to mean something… Something real. And if he was ready then she was too, but she had to know what he was feeling. Her words tumbled out in short breaths. 'If this isn't…if you can't…then please stop because I need more of you…'

He took her face in his hands. 'I can give you more…' Then he kissed her softly, deeply, and she was unravelling, losing herself in the perfect taste of his kiss, and when she thought she was about to die in his arms he pulled away breathlessly. 'Let's go home!'

She watched shadows weaving and dancing on the walls, felt his fingers tracing a slow, meandering journey along her inner arm, a sequence of little presses against her skin. She felt a glow of recognition. 'What are you playing?'

His lips touched her shoulder. '*Pavane*. You liked it, remember…?'

She rolled over to face him. His gaze was soft in the candlelight, hazy from their love-making. 'I don't know which one I like best… I love *Pavane*, but now there's the dirty dancing one…'

'The dirty dancing one!' He laughed. 'I'll never play *Gymnopédies* again without remembering…'

His gaze held a trace of heat, something else too which reached right into her heart and nestled there. She touched his shoulder, ran her fingers over the smooth arc of muscle. In this moment she felt so close to him, felt as if everything had opened up between them. The way he'd told her about Isabella, how they'd started out together…all that history…but there was something left, something she needed to know.

'Zach, what happened—to Isabella?'

She saw the light drain from his eyes, heard the little catch in his breath and then he was rolling onto his back. He stared at the ceiling for a long moment and she wondered if she'd pushed too hard, but then he started to speak.

'It was a brain haemorrhage—very sudden.'

She reached for his hand, felt him folding

it into his. He closed his eyes, as if it was the only way he could see into the past.

'We'd gone for dinner at friends'… It was a lovely evening so the plan was to eat outside. I was on the terrace with the guys, having a beer, and Izzy was inside, catching up with the girls. She was bringing a bowl of salad out and she must have caught the heel of her shoe somehow… I heard a crack, then a smash and when I looked up Izzy was on the ground… I ran over. For a moment she looked dazed, then she laughed, called herself a *klutz*. I helped her up. I was worried because she'd hit her head but she said she was fine, that it was just a bump. She was more worried about the broken salad bowl. She was picking up the pieces, apologising. I took her aside, asked her if she really was okay and she told me to stop worrying…'

He fell silent for a moment. Olivia felt his fingers tightening around hers.

'An hour later when we were eating, I felt her touch my hand suddenly, like she was trying to grab it, and then she collapsed, fell against me. I went crazy. I was holding her, calling her name, trying to wake her up, yelling for someone to get an ambulance, and it seemed to take for ever to come… They tried so hard to bring her back, but she didn't wake up again.'

Olivia tried to imagine it. One moment sitting there at the table, the next moment everything sliding away into darkness. Zach, floating in a vacuum of disbelief, the shock repeating like a mirror reflecting itself—on and on and on. She couldn't find the words so she squeezed his hand softly. 'Thank you for telling me.'

He turned to face her, traced the line of her jaw with his fingers. 'I've lived it a thousand times and every time it's the same. No warning. No time for saying…'

'Goodbye?'

He hesitated for a moment then nodded and as he looked at her she could see a glow there, kindling his eyes back to life.

'What do you say to Alessia…?'

He drew a wretched kind of sigh then seemed to steady himself. 'I put a photo of Izzy on her bedside table… I tell her that Mamma's with the angels, that she watches over her all the time, that she loves her…' He swallowed, shook his head a little. 'What can you say…? Alessia doesn't remember and maybe it's easier that way.' Lines appeared on his forehead. 'She sees the world with a child's eyes; she isn't burdened with sadness. If you have to lose a parent maybe it's easier if you never got to know them.'

He sat up suddenly, ran a hand through his hair. 'The only way I could think of to make Alessia feel Izzy's presence was to make this place everything Izzy had wanted it to be. Every piece of furniture, every paint colour... everything has Izzy's stamp on it. When Alessia's older maybe she'll feel her mother here somehow...' He picked up his watch from the bedside table and slipped it on, then swung out of bed, reaching for his trousers.

She sat up, holding the sheet against her body. 'You're not staying...?'

He turned around to face her. 'I'm sorry. Believe me, I want to—but I can't.' He was pulling on his shirt now, buttoning it up. 'Lucia's babysitting. I'm already later than I said I'd be.'

It was perfectly reasonable, so why did she feel a spike of desolation?

He pushed his feet into his shoes then came to sit beside her. He wrapped his arms around her, cool clothes against her warm skin. He kissed her softly. 'I'll see you tomorrow, okay.'

'Yes, of course...' She smiled. 'Sleep well, Zach.'

His eyes flickered with something she couldn't read, then he left the bedroom, closing the door quietly behind him.

She fell backwards and stared at the ceiling. He was in the east wing and she was in the west wing. Between them lay the house: everything with Isabella's stamp on it.

She took her coffee with her, walked barefoot through the dewy grass until she came to her favourite bench. There was a cool stillness in the garden, a peachy glow of dawn on the horizon. The day still felt like a figment of someone's imagination, like an idea not fully formed, and she wanted it to wash over her, clear her mind, suggest a direction.

The way he'd been last night…that slow dance, the way he'd held her against him, his hand at her back, fingers slowly circling… Just thinking about it, and what happened afterwards…the delicious heat of his skin against hers, slow, deep kisses, the ache of longing, the blissful ache of release… The sweet intimacy of it had stolen her breath away, otherwise she might have whispered her secret, told him that she was in love with him. She'd seen the light in his eyes too and she'd dared to hope… But then he'd left, and she'd had the whole night to think.

She sipped her coffee, stared at the old house glowing golden in the sunrise. It was his Taj Mahal, his monument to Isabella and a legacy for Alessia. It was unreasonable, illogical of her to feel threatened by it, but she couldn't switch off the feeling that this place would always stand between her and Zach. She felt the old demons awakening inside her—that yearning for total commitment, that yearning to be at the centre of someone's universe, not just a satellite passing through. And even though she could trace its origins to the thoughtless taunting she'd endured at school, and even though she'd learned that she had room in her heart for a widower with a daughter, somehow, the house and everything it stood for felt like too much. She'd never expect him to give it up— that would be selfish—but she needed something for herself. Some proof that she mattered as much—more. The problem was, she didn't know what that proof could be or how to find it.

The sun was climbing slowly, throwing shadows across the formal garden below. She got to her feet, wandered through the secret garden rooms she loved. Pale statues, enigmatic smiles. She ran her fingers over the smooth cold arm of a cherub and fought back a wave of sadness. Her time here was running out. Two more weddings to shoot and then Michele would be well enough to come back. So many things crowding into her head at once. What would happen in two weeks? What did she want to happen? Her feelings for Zach were undeniable, but this thing they'd started…was it all just a massive mistake? Was he going to shake her hand at the airport and say goodbye?

'You're up early!'

Startled, she looked up to see Lucia strolling towards her through the stone archway of the ancient folly. She was wearing a light summer dress and sandals, a cardigan draped over her shoulders.

Olivia tightened the belt of her robe, felt its wet hemline catching her ankles. 'I woke up early. Couldn't go back to sleep.' She smiled. 'I thought I might as well come outside.'

Lucia's eyes held her in a warm gaze. 'Ah! Well, it's the best time of day for a walk. So quiet, so cool. I always find it a good time for thinking about things…'

Olivia saw a glint in the older woman's eye, remembered Zach telling her how Lucia had seemed *a little unsettled* about her being here. Strange! Apart from the very first time they'd met, she'd never found Lucia to be anything other than warm and friendly. It flitted through her mind that perhaps it had been Zach himself who'd felt unsettled. She looked down at her feet, gave a little shrug. 'I wasn't expecting to bump into anyone…'

Lucia waved a dismissive hand, chuckled. 'It's fine! There was a time I'd walk barefoot in the grass too.' She brushed an insect off her shoulder. 'How was your dinner?'

'It was…lovely.' She felt a blush creeping over her cheeks. Lucia had been babysitting last night, would have been there when Zach got back—very late. 'The hotel is magnificent—we had a balcony table, a thousand feet above the sea.'

'Ambruosi's very famous and of course the gardens are delightful.' She plucked a bougainvillea blossom from a swinging stem, twirled it in her fingers. 'It was nice to see Zach going out on a date… He works too much.'

Olivia felt a swell of gratitude followed by a crushing desire to cry. The older woman seemed to be bestowing a kind of blessing on her. In the wake of her uncharitable feelings about Isabella, how thwarted she'd been feeling by Isabella's invisible presence, it was humbling. She swallowed hard. 'Yes! He does.'

'You've got two more weddings, two more weeks with us, yes?'

Olivia nodded.

'It'll be gone before you know it.'

She nodded again, folded and unfolded

her arms. 'I was thinking the same thing this morning.' She felt her lips wobbling into a lopsided grin. 'Feeling a bit sad about it, you know.'

Lucia swished past her then turned around, fixed her with a level gaze. 'You must make the most of the time you have… That's all any of us can ever do.' She smiled. 'Enjoy the rest of your walk.'

Olivia stared after her until she'd disappeared from view and then she wrapped her arms around herself and walked slowly towards the stone arch. Lucia seemed to be encouraging her—to do what—get closer to Zach? She leaned against the cool stone and sealed her eyes shut. It wasn't that easy, especially when she was on the verge of thinking that last night had been a terrible mistake… She'd wanted him so much, but she should have thought it through a bit more. What had happened between them hadn't felt like a casual thing, but what it was exactly she didn't know and, until she did, she couldn't let it happen again.

Such a mess!

She took a deep breath and opened her eyes. Maybe he'd say something, tell her he wanted her to stay…and then at least she'd have something to work with.

If he didn't say anything—she sucked in another deep breath—if he didn't, then maybe she'd have to keep in mind what Lucia had just said about time. Her last two weeks were going to fly by. Maybe she should stop worrying about where things might go with Zach... Maybe she needed to dig out some of her old resilience, concentrate on getting out more, seeing things, having fun. Two weeks left— she had to make them count.

CHAPTER NINE

ZACH WATCHED OLIVIA squinting at the screen of her mobile, her face contorting with concentration. 'I don't know why you're bothering—you'll find it on Google Images. It's the most photographed tree in the whole of Italy, apparently.'

She tapped the screen, frowned, tapped it again. 'Rightly so! It's magnificent and completely lovely. As to why I'm bothering—I just want my own souvenir of the Rufolo umbrella tree. At least I'm not dragging you into a selfie.' She looked at him, a flicker of uncertainty in her eyes, and then she turned away to look at the view. 'I can't get over how blue that sea is.'

'Hopefully, it'll cheer up soon.'

'Ha ha, very funny!' She pocketed her phone then stepped close, wrapped her arms around his waist and huffed a little sigh. 'I keep thinking I should've brought the proper camera but after yesterday—ugh! Just the thought of tugging that thing about in this heat—'

'You need a break.' He kissed the tip of her nose. 'Ready to move on?'

'Yes! What's next?'

He slung an arm around her shoulders, started walking. 'The gardens at Villa Cimbrone. The Terrace of Infinity.'

She peeked at him from under her sunglasses. 'It sounds very romantic.'

'It'll be heaving with *turisti*—'

'Of which I am one.' She mock-frowned, quirking her lovely mouth. 'Is it painful, doing the tourist thing with me…? It's just that I want to see everything before I leave.'

Before I leave.

Her words struck him like a body blow, but he smiled. 'Of course I don't mind. You know I like…being with you.'

'Ditto.' She smiled then looked away.

He steered her back through the gardens, past the Moorish Tower with its famous fresco and along a shady path which led back to the Piazza Centrale, then he took her hand and led her through the crowds towards Cimbrone.

He couldn't believe that over a week had passed since they'd had dinner at the hotel, since they'd danced on that twinkling walkway, since they'd made love for the first—and only—time. He'd been mesmerised that evening, had felt so close to her, so…*found*.

But something had changed. She'd started speaking to him in exclamation marks. Colourful, upbeat tones, the joviality in her voice never quite reaching her eyes. Yet when he touched her she melted into him just like before, and when he kissed her he knew her truth. She wanted something from him, and the imminence of her departure was making everything worse.

After yesterday's wedding, her penultimate, he'd hoped for a quiet day but she'd asked him to take her sightseeing in Ravello because *'I'll be leaving soon'*. Lucia had told her she ought to see the gardens at Rufolo and Cimbrone, and they were the last places he wanted to go because of the crowds and because Izzy had loved the gardens so much.

As he dodged and weaved through the ambling tourists, pulling her along in his wake, he was fighting the urge to sit her down in some quiet bar, tell her he'd fallen in love with her. But what would he say after that? When he imagined the scene it was the part that always tripped him up. Falling in love with her was easy, but he wasn't a free agent. He was tied to the business, and there was Alessia to think about. If she wanted to be with him she'd have to slot into this life he'd made, take on his daughter, and he wasn't at all sure if that was what she really wanted. And there was something else too...

He still dreamed about Izzy. Did that mean he hadn't let go enough? How could he know how much letting go was enough? It wasn't as if he'd been a widower before. He had no experience of how grief worked. There seemed to be an aching gap between himself and the person he wanted to be, and he didn't know how to bridge it. Most importantly, he didn't want to hurt Olivia, so he'd followed her lead—kept things light and breezy—but it didn't feel real and it was killing him. He *had* to talk to her, find a way somehow. In the meantime, he was condemned to plodding beside her on the narrow pathway to the gardens behind a group of shuffling tourists. He watched her feet, tuned in to the soft slap of her sandals on the stone path.

When they struck a patch of shade she pushed her sunglasses up. 'Lucia was telling me that the Bloomsbury Set used to come to Villa Cimbrone.'

More chit-chat.

'That's right! It's attracted a lot of artistic types over the years.' He threw her a smile.

'Greta Garbo stayed here back in the thirties, but she didn't come *"alone"*!'

'You're on fire today!' She was laughing, that familiar warm light shining in her eyes, and for a moment everything felt perfect.

He put on a tour guide voice. 'The gardens were extended and improved in the early twentieth century by Ernest William Beckett. In later life, he was saddled with the unfortunate title of Lord Grimthorpe but, on the bright side, he *was* a friend of Vita Sackville-West, so he probably got a bit of free gardening advice... how to prune his roses—'

She was properly laughing now, dimples in her cheeks, eyes shining. Her face looked so sweet and happy that he couldn't help laughing too. 'I've probably got all that wrong. Izzy was the one who knew...'

Her laughter faded and the glow in her eyes dimmed a little bit. He cursed under his breath. He'd have to stop doing that...mentioning... and yet he couldn't switch Izzy off like a tap. She'd been a massive part of his life. Maybe coming here had been a mistake, but Ravello was a small town; there wasn't much in it that he hadn't seen or experienced with his wife.

They queued at the kiosk, sun beating down. She pulled on a sunhat. He wished he'd remembered to bring one. He paid, shoved the tickets into his pocket. He showed her the cloisters, watched her taking in the pale stone arches, the mullions twisted like sticks of barley sugar. The courtyard space was filled with glinting sun, pockets of shade. Ivy grasped at the walls, reaching past other climbers which he couldn't name.

On the Terrace of Infinity she gazed at the view, examined the busts, giggled at one with a broken snub nose. He watched boats streaking across the sea, remembered kissing her for the first time. She stuck her feet through the railings at the lookout point, gazed down at the scalloped terraces and tiny white houses. 'You should try this—it makes you feel dizzy!'

You make me feel dizzy.

He led her along a covered walkway, wishing the wisteria was still in bloom so she could see it, the clusters of petals rippling like confetti. On through the rose garden, heady with scent, past statues to the Temple of Bacchus, then more paths, worn steps and everywhere splashes of colour, fat, bristling yew trees, slender cypresses and the tall umbrella pines.

On the lawn she took out her phone, aimed it at the view and tutted. 'I know *I'm* a tourist so I have no right to get impatient, but I *wish* all these people would vanish so I can get a clean shot.'

He wished all the people would vanish too. He stepped behind her, wrapped his arms around her shoulders. She sank back against him, warm and damp. He kissed her neck, tasted the saltiness of her skin. 'I think we should find a quiet bar, grab a cold one...'

She swivelled to look at him, a wicked gleam in her eye. 'You mean you're not enjoying the *turisti*?'

'I want to get out of here—' he released her, grabbed her hand '—and I'm taking you with me!' He started running across the lawn and she was running beside him, holding onto her hat, laughing. Then she was tugging at his hand, breathless, giggling.

'Zach, stop! What about the gift shop?'

He looked back, saw that she was teasing and pulled her on. 'Don't even think about it!'

Off the main drag, away from the crowds, he spotted an arched doorway, heavy doors pinned back with iron bolts, black and white floor tiles. A big green pot plant squatted in the entrance lobby, its fronds disturbed by the slight breeze. It looked cool, inviting but, most importantly, it was unfamiliar.

'This place looks promising.'

She pushed her sunglasses up, smiled. 'Okay.'

The interior was unexpected. A domed skylight in a high ceiling funnelled light into the centre of the room but the light fell away sharply so that the tables clustered around the walls were crushed into semi-darkness, brightened only a little by the tea lights flickering in amber glass lanterns. More amber lanterns were suspended at intervals over the long mahogany bar, and at the end of the bar, in a corner, gleamed a baby grand.

'Where is everybody?' Olivia's voice was hushed.

He'd been about to say the same thing. The place was deserted. He squeezed her hand, called out, 'Hello? Is there anybody here—?'

So quiet. He let go of her hand, walked to the bar and called out again. No reply. He looked at the piano, wandered over, lifted the lid carefully. He pressed middle C, heard the note ring out clear and true. He smiled. He hadn't touched a piano in quite a while. He tried a scale.

Nice!

'You play the piano too?' She was walking towards him, eyes curious.

He ran a hand through his hair, smiled. 'A bit. I had lessons—it's how I started really. Then I got into guitars and left the old Joanna behind.' He played a few one-handed notes. '*This* is a lovely instrument.'

'Play something—please.' She was smiling. Properly happy.

He pulled out the stool and sat down, tested the pedals. It had been so long since he'd played. He looked at her, lifted an eyebrow. 'This might well be a catastrophe...' Then he ran his fingers over the keys, took a deep breath.

Focus.

The first notes sounded clumsy, and then it came back. *Für Elise*, his grade seven piece, the notes rising and falling, that moment of teetering on a brink then filling out, swelling into the bolder melody. He glanced up. She'd rested her cheek into her hand, in her eyes a look of... He looked down, watched his fingers on the keys, losing himself...

As he played the final note a voice ballooned through the room. 'Bravo!'

Startled, he swung round, jumped to his feet. Behind the bar stood a middle-aged man, slightly balding, with dark eyes, grey smudges underneath, a gap between his two front teeth.

'Thanks! I hope you don't mind. We came in for a drink, but there was no one...' He shrugged. 'I saw the piano...'

'It's absolutely fine! I just opened up, then

had to go out for a moment. I'm sorry I wasn't here.' He smiled. 'I'm Marcello. What can I get you?'

Zach looked at Olivia.

'Frascati, please.' She smiled. 'And a glass of cold water.'

'I'll have the same, thanks.'

Marcello reached for glasses, twisted the caps off two bottles of water and set them on a tray.

Zach stepped up to the bar, pulled out his wallet. 'It's funny, I haven't noticed this place before. Have you just opened?'

Marcello's eyes snapped up. 'Yes. Last week.' He poured two glasses of wine.

'Ah…' Zach looked around. It had a nice vibe, a bit different to the other bars he knew. 'It's great!'

Marcello put the wine glasses onto the tray. 'It is—although, sadly, I might have to give it up.'

'Why?' Olivia had parked her elbows on the bar.

Marcello glanced at her then looked at Zach. 'Let's just say that my brother let me down. We were supposed to be business partners.'

Olivia frowned. 'I'm sorry. That's terrible.'

Marcello shrugged. 'Where would you like to sit?'

Zach looked around, pointed to a random table. He was curious about Marcello's predicament but he didn't want to press him. 'So, do you play the piano?'

Marcello laughed roundly. 'No! It's my brother who plays but we wanted to have a piano in the bar, for people to play if they want… You play very well…er…?'

'Zach! I'm sorry. I should have introduced myself. This is Olivia.'

Marcello nodded at Olivia then decanted their glasses and water bottles onto the table. 'It's nice to meet you both.'

A group of four were drifting in. Marcello acknowledged them with a nod then turned back to Zach. 'Let me know if you need anything else, and please—if you want to play the piano again, feel free.'

'Thanks!'

When he turned to face Olivia he found her watching him with a bemused expression on her face. He picked up his glass, smiled. 'What—?'

'Just you.'

'Me?'

She took a drink of water then picked up her wine glass. 'You love playing so much. I could watch you all day.'

He laughed. 'Hmm—I think the novelty would soon wear off.'

'Why do you always do that?' She was frowning at him.

'Do what?'

She leaned forward on her elbows, fixed him in her gaze. 'Whenever you talk about your music, you downplay it. You say you *dabble,* or that you played *little gigs.* Or you say you were *deluding yourself.* What's that all about?'

He drank from his glass, let the cool wine slip down and hit the sweet spot. 'It's terminology, that's all.'

'What did Isabella think about your playing?'

'She—' He drew a momentary blank, shrugged. 'I was finished with music when I met her. I was ready to move on. I didn't play much. We had other things going on.'

She sat back in her chair and sipped her wine. He wished he could see what she was thinking. He'd wanted to have a heart to heart but playing the piano for her seemed to have jinxed everything.

'Liv, you mustn't read too much into the music thing…' He leaned across the table, held her in his gaze. 'I love music. I always have, I always will, and I do think about it sometimes, but it's a cruel business and being good isn't enough. You need to be lucky, connected maybe, you need to give up everything and even if you do that there's no guarantee of success. By the time the band split I was happy enough to walk away, to move on with my life. Maybe my dreams of rock superstardom died, but other dreams came true. I fell in love, made a home in Italy, had a beautiful daughter and then...'

I fell in love with you.

He held the words in his mouth, rolled them around on his tongue. Somehow, this didn't feel like the right moment.

'And then?'

He shrugged, moistened his lips. 'And then the dreams change.' He grinned. 'You dream of cold Frascati in a quiet bar, a dip in the sea with your daughter—stuff like that.'

He watched her gazing around.

'Well, whatever you say, I can see something in you when you're playing that feels... I don't know...like you're at home in your skin.' She turned, met his eyes, her expression soft. 'Have you ever thought about something like this?'

'What do you mean?'

'Like running your own music bar?' She smiled. 'I think you'd be in your element, being around musicians more, playing gigs yourself, bringing guest musicians in. Ravello's the city of music, after all!'

He shook his head. It was a ludicrous idea. He was too busy with Casa Isabella to even consider it, and there was the new venue his father wanted him to find.

He glanced at the piano then drained his glass. 'In another life, maybe. In this one, I've been tasked with finding a second wedding venue on the Amalfi Coast. A new sister for Casa Isabella. Merrill Hotels is expanding its Italian interests! How about another drink?'

She shook her head. 'No—no, thanks.' There was something in her eyes. She seemed upset. 'I... Do you mind if I abandon you for a little while...?'

'I thought we were having a drink...?' Suddenly it felt as if everything was crashing around his ears. 'Is it something I said?'

She was reaching for her bag, standing up. 'No, nothing like that. It's just that I wanted to get some postcards and some tourist trash to take home.'

He couldn't let her leave. He started to stand up. 'I'll come with you...'

'No!' She put out a hand to stop him. 'You'd hate it, poking around crowded shops.' She glanced at the piano. 'You should stay here, play some more... I'll be back soon.'

She didn't give him time to reply, just turned away and hurried towards the door.

The light outside seemed too bright. It was prickling her eyes, making them water, or maybe it wasn't the light. She slipped on her sunglasses and walked quickly down the narrow street towards the town centre.

Why was everything such a mess?

The morning after their dinner date, after they'd been so tender with each other, he'd been tied up with meetings and when they did see each other he hadn't said anything about wanting her to stay on after her wedding shoots were finished, so she'd decided to be light and breezy about everything, not wanting him to think that she expected anything—and the whole week had felt weird, and today had been weird too. There'd been moments when things had felt normal, but at other times...

She stopped walking, fell back against a shady wall. The problem was they were skating around a conversation they needed to have, stuck in a pathetic limbo because neither of them wanted to say *What happens now?*

What happens now?

That he could play the piano had been a revelation. She loved watching him, listening to him, the way he seemed to become this other person, as if the music was freeing him. And when he'd looked up at her something in his eyes had made her ache with longing, reminded her of how intimate they'd been, how much she wanted to feel that closeness again.

And then, as she'd looked around the bar, it had come to her that his music was her proof. She loved his playing, treasured it like a precious thing, because it was all him, the purest expression of his spirit, the thing about him that had nothing to do with Isabella or the growing aspirations of Merrill Hotels. She wasn't asking him to forget anything in his past but she wanted some part of him that was hers alone to take forward into the future. And so she'd suggested a music bar.

'In another life, maybe.'

His words had cut her down, because that was exactly what she wanted. She wanted him to have another life, not this one where he was married to Casa Isabella, sidelining his talent, enduring long Sunday phone calls with his father. She wanted to hear him play his music, she wanted him to have time for paddling pool afternoons with Alessia, for making pizza from scratch, for dancing...

She pushed herself away from the wall and

walked on. But how could she say those things to him? She had no claim on him, no say in how he lived his life. They'd spent a night together—not even a whole night—and the next morning it was as if too much time had passed and there'd been a gap between them that should have been filled with light and love and laughter, but wasn't.

In the town centre she crossed the *piazza*, wandered through the crowded alleys on the other side, past little shops and bars. She stopped to take a photo of some grapefruit-sized lemons in a basket, all pale and knobbly. Her dad would have laughed, would have picked one up to feel the weight of it. She squeezed into a busy gift shop, bought postcards—a nice one of the 'most photographed tree in Italy' with that blue sea beyond. Others of pretty pastel towns teetering on craggy cliffs. Several of the Cimbrone Gardens, then some random views: narrow streets with peeling doors...the cathedral. Pictures she would have taken for herself if she'd brought her proper camera. In another shop she bought souvenir bottles of Limoncello and a leather purse for her mum, then she retraced her steps to the *piazza* and sat on the warm cathedral steps with a hundred other tourists.

She gazed across the square, remembered

the first night she'd seen it—the cafés and bars
all closed, Zach fidgety because she hadn't said
anything about his playing. It had mattered so
much to him what she thought, and now he
was trying to convince her that his music had
been a young man's dream, something he'd
cast aside quite happily. She didn't believe him.

She pulled out her phone, looked at the photo
of the giant lemons. Idly, she drew eyes on
them, little shocked mouths, added a caption:
Massive mutant lemons caught in the wild!
She thought about her dad again, what he'd
said about bringing her up to be a free spirit.
She'd felt like a free spirit when he'd been there
for her, watching her back, and then, after he
left, she'd turned into this other person. A person who needed everything to be squared off,
a person who was uncomfortable with loose
ends. Someone who was frightened to speak
out. She turned the phone over and over in
her hands. Her parents had been wrong not
to include her in their decision to separate but
maybe she'd been too hard on them, too hard
on her dad especially. He was only human; everyone made mistakes. She'd made hers, with
Zach.

Her dad was just at the other end of the
phone if she needed him, probably up to his
oxters in a river, but there all the same and

thinking about that made her feel better. She attached the silly lemons photo to a text and sent it to him. What would he think when he got it? He'd be pleased. Maybe he'd feel a change in her—sense a return of the old Liv. She wondered what he'd advise her to do about Zach. He'd probably shrug, say he was the last person to ask and she'd laugh and tell him he was right. Her phone buzzed. He'd texted back! Laughing icon, thumbs-up icon, blowing kiss icon. Three symbols which felt like diamonds in her hand—symbols which proved that he was right there if she needed him. She swallowed a little sob of relief, wiped her eyes under her sunglasses.

Zach would be wondering where she was. Imagining his eyes, his smile, she drew in a long, slow breath. She'd taken a wrong turn after her conversation with Lucia in the garden that morning. Instead of talking to Zach, she'd buried her head in the sand, turned into an avatar, some upbeat version of herself—a sightseer, for goodness' sake!

She picked up her bags, threaded her way down the steps through the tourists sitting enjoying the late-afternoon sun.

Telling Zach what was in her heart wouldn't be easy—she might well lose him—but she couldn't put it off any longer. In a week she'd be shooting her last wedding and a few days after that she'd be leaving. She needed to talk to him. Ask the question: *What happens now?*

Her phone buzzed—Zach was texting.

Where are you?

She tapped out a reply.

On my way.

She walked along the narrow street, past the pale lemon walls of a smart hotel then onwards into a narrow pedestrian alley with grey crumbly-looking walls. In front of her a small knot of tourists melted away and then she saw him leaning against a wall, his phone in his hand. When he spotted her his eyebrows lifted and he broke into a smile—a smile that made her heart quicken.

'Did you get what you wanted?'

'Yeah…'

He was searching her face, his eyes so clear and blue, so intense, that she wanted to look away, or fall into his arms. She fiddled with the bag in her hand, wondering how to begin, when suddenly he said, 'Liv, we need to talk.'

She swallowed hard, met his gaze again. 'Yes.'

Silently, he took her hand, led her up the walkway and into a small public garden which overlooked the sea. There was a green bench with a curved back, happily vacant. He sat down and she sat beside him. It was a sheltered spot. The late afternoon sun was throwing long shadows, playing with texture in the pale stone walls and in the leaves, and the grass and the railings.

He released her hand, smiled awkwardly. 'Where to begin…?'

She looked at him, tried to read the tiny fluctuations of light in his eyes, watched him drawing in a breath and letting it out again.

He ran a hand through his hair. 'I want to say sorry for the other night… I should never have—'

'You regret what happened?' The words had sprung from her mouth—defensive. She could feel her heart going fast.

Breathe.

'No!' He shook his head. 'You must never think that.' His eyes softened. 'Olivia, my feelings for you… It's not a question of regret… But I didn't think things through. Leaving you afterwards—it felt so wrong, but I had to get back for Alessia, and then the next day I wanted to talk to you, but you seemed different. All week you've been different, and

I haven't known what to say to you or what you're expecting from me.'

'Expecting?' She looked at her fingers. 'You make it sound as if everything's down to me.'

'Liv, please look at me.'

She lifted her eyes to his.

'Can't you see that I'm in love with you?' The light in his eyes, enfolding her, making her heart stop and start and quicken. 'But I'm worried that I'm not what you want. I'm a fixed entity. I have a business, a child, a life here—' He reached his hand to her face, stroked her cheekbone with his thumb. She felt her senses swimming, an ache of longing building deep inside. 'I never expected to feel this way about anyone again and I'm floundering because where we go from here is up to you.'

A little breeze caressed her neck and it seemed to steady her. 'I don't think it's up to me, Zach.' She lifted his hand away from her cheek. 'You say you're a fixed entity, but none of us is fixed.'

She turned her gaze to the sea, examined the blur of sea and sky on the horizon. 'For a long time I had this fixed idea about what I wanted in a relationship. A perfect love, starting out together, all the boxes ticked. No loose ends. The opposite of my parents. And then you came along and all those rigid ideas of what makes perfection started to crumble. My frame widened.' She turned to face him. 'I was falling in love with you, then I discovered I had room in my heart for Alessia as well.'

He was looking at her intently, eyes filling with a hazy kind of light.

'But one thing hasn't changed. I don't like uncertainty. I want commitment and I don't know if you can give me that.' He opened his mouth to speak but she had to finish. 'You say you're in love with me, but how can you be in love with me when you haven't said goodbye to Isabella?'

'Izzy's gone—'

'She's gone, yes, but at the same time she's everywhere.' She felt tears gathering behind her eyes, swallowed hard. 'On your boat, at Villa Cimbrone today. She's probably here in these gardens too... At the house, every colour on every wall, every piece of furniture—her choice. And I understand, I really do. Surrounding Alessia with all the things her mother loved... I wouldn't have expected anything less from a devoted father. But you must see that you're wrong about everything being up to me.' She saw his eyes cloud. 'What

I want, what I need from you is something that feels like a beginning.'

'So you want me to…what—put the past behind me?' He slumped backwards. 'I can't do that. Izzy's inside me—she'll always be there.'

'I'm not asking you to forget the past, or your wife—I would never ask you to do that—but I need to feel that you can widen your frame too. Go forward…'

He was shaking his head. 'How?'

'I'm talking about—' she couldn't bring herself to mention his music again '—being true to yourself. You joined the family business to make your father happy, you bought a wedding venue because Isabella was ambitious, and you've devoted yourself to making it everything she wanted it to be and more. And I'm not saying that those were bad decisions, that you weren't happy to make them at the time, but the look on your face when you told me about the new wedding venue—it wasn't the look of a man who wants to build a wedding empire.'

He held her gaze then looked away across the sea.

'You're holding on so tightly, Zach, and I don't know why. You won't hand things over to a manager, not even so you can spend more time with Alessia, and if you won't do it for your daughter there's no hope for me. If you can't let go of your old life then I can't build a new one with you.'

He turned to face her, eyes more grey than blue, shut down somehow. 'So that's it then.'

CHAPTER TEN

THE ROAD WAS quieter than he'd thought it would be and he was glad. Driving the coastal route towards Sorrento could be slow. It was usually clogged with tourist buses and local traffic, pedestrians walking, shrinking back as impatient scooters zipped through gaps. Carefully, he passed a line of dusty cars parked tightly against the kerb, impossibly close to one another, dents and scrapes in doors and wings. He accelerated out of the town, felt a flicker of elation.

Driving! This sensation of forward motion, of clearing the bends and twists in the road with the sea at his shoulder and the sun on his face was exactly what he needed after days behind his desk, working with his father on the viability of a new wedding venue. He'd hardly seen Olivia. She'd cloistered herself away, editing, and he'd kept his distance because he couldn't think of what to say to her.

He'd felt bruised by her words in the Giardini Principessa di Piemonte. Chastened because she was right about Izzy being everywhere. He'd stood in those same gardens with Izzy, his arms wrapped around her, watching the sun sliding into the sea. And when she'd said, *'You haven't said goodbye to Isabella'*, she'd unwittingly hit another nerve. A sigh shuddered through him. Losing someone so suddenly left no time for goodbyes, left no time for saying all the things you should have said, like—*I'm sorry.*

He'd told Olivia what happened the night Izzy died, but he hadn't told her everything. He hadn't told her that on the way over to their friends' house they'd had a disagreement about a fountain for the garden. He hadn't flat out refused, but what Izzy had wanted was out of budget—although he'd bought Casa Dorato, Merrill Hotels was funding the renovation and he was under pressure to prioritise the internal work so they could start forward booking. They'd both been overtired—Alessia had been teething for weeks, waking them up at night. In the car, things had got a little heated and when they arrived they'd gone their separate ways. Him onto the terrace for a beer with his friends, Izzy into the house to chat to hers. And then she'd brought out the salad.

After the funeral the first thing he did was put in the fountain, and then he'd kept going—doing everything she'd wanted. Trying to make amends. Guilt and sorrow bound up with atonement. It was a hard habit to break, but if he didn't want to lose Olivia he would have to try.

For days he'd been thinking about all the things she'd said, and she was right: building a wedding empire wasn't his dream, but it was his family's business and if Merrill Hotels wanted to expand then he was obliged to facilitate that. It was why he was making this trip—to view a prospective acquisition.

At a junction he took a right and drove up a steep winding road until he arrived at a pair of stone pillars. A black sign with gold lettering confirmed that he was in the right place: *Villa Fiori*. He liked the look of the entrance: classy enough for Merrill Select. As he drove down the long shady driveway and parked the car he felt a lightening of spirit. Maybe running two venues would give him the push he needed, compel him to delegate the day-to-day running of things in both venues, and that would give him more time for Alessia. More time for living.

Villa Fiori was completely different from Casa Isabella. The manager, Lorenzo, was very accommodating and showed him around with pride. It was a modern boutique hotel with pale marble floors, lots of glass and chrome—the kind of thing that Milo might have designed. The sea views were spectacular, the bedrooms and bathrooms large and luxurious. The function room had a glass ceiling and shutters which opened onto a terrace laid with wooden decking, sheltered from the wind by glass panels, stainless-steel rails running along the top. Zach liked the contemporary vibe, could see the kind of clients who would be attracted to such a place.

The manager left him to go ahead and look at the grounds on his own. There was a large rectangular formal garden, well laid out with areas of cool shade under the mature trees. Olivia would know how to improve it for photography and thinking about her made him realise how much he was missing her, how much he liked being with her. He wondered what she was doing at that moment. Was she thinking about him? He felt a stab of anguish and walked on.

There was an old lemon grove adjacent to the main garden, a suggestion in the sales particulars that the land could be developed for guest chalets or a gymnasium, but he already knew that if he bought Villa Fiori he would never destroy the lemon grove. He'd never shaken off the Englishman's thrill of seeing lemons dangling from branches and as he walked through the trees, treading a path through a froth of groundcover, he thought about his wedding day… They'd got married in a place just like this. He looked up into the branches, caught little glimpses of the blue sky above, and for a moment he could feel the shape of her hand in his, see her eyes shining for him, full of love.

They'd written their own vows. He'd made his pledge to her in Italian; she'd spoken to him in her faltering English. *'We will make mistakes, Zach, and there will be days which are not easy but I vow that, whatever happens, I will hold you in my heart for ever.'*

He swallowed hard, pictured her face, the way she'd look at him with her sweet secret smile. He closed his eyes, listened to the sound of his own breathing and the sound of the leaves rustling in the breeze.

And I'll hold you in my heart for ever too, Izzy… I'm sorry we never got the chance to say goodbye, but I have to say it now. I've got to start again… I think I've been given a second chance, and I've got to find a way to take it.

'So, you think it's an option?'

'Definitely! It's classy, well maintained, well

situated and it's completely different to what we've got so we'll be widening our client base.'

'I like the sound of that. What about the lemon grove, the potential?'

'Forget it! If we're selling weddings, the lemon grove's an asset. It needs tidying up, but with some TLC it'll give us another option for the ceremony. We can make all the outdoor spaces flow together. That means maximum flexibility in terms of what we can offer our clients.'

'You don't think guest chalets—?'

'No, Dad! If we buy Villa Fiori, the lemon grove stays. It's special! And we don't need guest chalets—there are twenty-eight bedrooms!'

'Okay.' Cynical sigh. 'If you say so. What about staff?'

'The manager thinks the staff will stay.'

'Will *he* stay?'

'Yes. I spoke to him about that. He's doing a great job there. He's invaluable and he knows it. If we buy the place, I suggest we give him a salary increase to keep him sweet—I'd be in trouble if he decided to leave.'

'Fine! Right then, I'll instruct our people to make an offer and we'll see what happens. Have a safe drive back, son!'

'I will. Bye, Dad.'

Zach stared at the phone in his hand, felt a little wash of relief. If the sale went through his father would get the business expansion he wanted, and if Lorenzo stayed on as manager his own role at Villa Fiori would be minor once the restructuring from hotel to wedding venue had been achieved. And he'd saved the lemon grove, at least for now.

He rolled the phone around in his hands, then tapped the screen, opened his photos. Olivia on the boat. He felt his lips twitching upwards into a smile. Her face tense with concentration then laughing, clowning about, doing Jack Sparrow... They'd narrowly missed that marker but it had felt so great, just having fun, and he wanted to feel like that again, make things right somehow. If only there was a way to show her... He closed the screen, threw his phone onto the passenger seat and started the engine.

The drive back to Ravello was slow. Outside Praiano, traffic was tailing back from the tunnel. He switched on the sound system, listened to Pablo Sáinz Villegas playing the adagio from Rodrigo's *Concierto de Aranjuez*.

He remembered an interview he'd seen, Pablo talking about music being an extension of his soul, an expression of his spirit, and he could hear it in every note Villegas was playing, could relate so strongly to that feeling. He shifted in his seat. What had Olivia said to him in Marcello's bar? *'I can see something in you when you're playing that feels… I don't know… like you're at home in your skin.'*

He smiled, remembering the way she'd watched him playing in the bar that first time, tears welling in her eyes when he'd played Fauré's *Pavane*…and afterwards on the street, her expression so soft and earnest… *'I'm not qualified to know if you're up to playing Carnegie Hall, but I can see how much you love music and I think that's why you feel restless after a gig…'*

That she'd been moved by his playing had touched him deeply, had made him want to kiss her, fuse his spirit with hers. He shifted in his seat again, realised he was chewing his thumb nail. The way he felt on Thursday afternoons—looking forward to playing. It was only a little set in a little bar but playing freed him in a way that nothing else did, and she could see it, had seen in it in him straight away. *'You should do more with it, chase the thing you love…'*

The traffic was moving now and as the car crawled through the tunnel he was breathing in fumes and Pablo's haunting guitar was echoing all around him and thoughts were flying through his head so fast that he almost couldn't keep up. As he drove out of the tunnel into the fresh air and blinding sunshine everything fell into place.

Liv wanted commitment, but she wanted something for him too. He could see it now— what she'd been trying to say. *'I'm talking about being true to yourself...'*

She wanted him to free himself—through his music. Not because she wanted him to forget Izzy or the past, but because she felt the greatest connection with him when he was playing—that was where she wanted them to begin. He'd been so blind. In Marcello's bar she'd even suggested he could run a similar place and he'd dismissed the idea out of hand. He'd upset her! That was why she'd left so suddenly.

This was something he could fix but words wouldn't be enough. He needed to make her feel it, needed to make a grand gesture…and then suddenly he couldn't stop himself from smiling because he knew exactly what he was going to do.

Olivia stared at the cardboard box on her bed. It had arrived a couple of days ago. She knew what was inside but she hadn't been able to face opening it until now. She cut through the plastic binder and slid the inner box from its cardboard sleeve. Slowly, she lifted the lid, felt a little gasp escaping from her lips. It was perfect. A whitewashed oak frame, four photographs side by side in sequence. Zach and Alessia singing the ant song! Animated faces, shining eyes and, in the last photo, eyes half-closed, both of them laughing hard. Just one of many happy memories of her Italian summer.

She closed the box, pressed her palms to her eyes. She hadn't seen much of him since their sightseeing day in Ravello. Instead of bringing them closer together, their talk in the gardens had driven a wedge between them. She'd been over their conversation a hundred times in her head, realised how intractable she'd sounded, as if she was delivering an ultimatum. She hadn't meant to sound that way. When she'd said that she couldn't build a new life with him if he was hanging onto the old one it had been more a statement of fact than anything else, but he'd clammed up after that and they'd driven home nursing a troubled silence.

In the house he'd taken her hands in his, kissed her on the cheek then walked down the hallway towards his apartment. There'd been finality in that kiss, the sense of a wall between them that she couldn't breach. She'd turned and walked down the opposite hallway to her own rooms, crying the whole way.

East. West. The house in between.

When she'd cried herself out, it came to her that at least she'd spoken her mind, told Zach what she needed, and there was something in that realisation that gave her strength. Whatever happened next would be down to him, and in the meantime there was work to do.

But work didn't stop her heart aching, didn't stop her missing his smile. She took to meandering around the house, hoping to run into him, but he was never around. In a bolder moment she'd run upstairs to his office, was about to knock on his door when she'd heard his voice and realised that he was on the phone. She'd retreated, taken herself for a walk in the garden and bumped into Lucia. Lucia had told her he was busy making plans for a new wedding venue and the news had lowered her spirits.

Perhaps she'd got him all wrong! Maybe he *was* a businessman above everything else and she'd been reading things into his music because it was the only toehold she could find, the only piece of him that didn't belong to Isabella.

If he was going ahead with a new wedding venue it meant he was choosing business over music; it meant that if she wanted to be part of his world she would have to fit in. She tried to imagine it but drew a blank. She would never be happy, never feel important enough if she was just another card slotted into the pack.

She picked up the cardboard box. The walls in his apartment were bare, pictures waiting to be hung. Perhaps he would put this one up at least. She'd take it to him. If he was there, maybe they could mend their fences, agree to be friends.

There was a heavy stillness in the house. A hush in the hallway. She tuned in to a far-off noise in the garden—a wheelbarrow moving over gravel. She could feel her heart drumming against her ribs, her stomach churning. If she was resigned to being just friends, then why was her heart beating double time at the thought of seeing him?

She stopped at his door, swallowed hard and knocked. She heard a door bang somewhere but it hadn't come from inside. The apartment was deadly quiet. She licked her lips and knocked again, harder this time, straining to hear any movement inside, but there was nothing. Deflated, she turned around and froze.

He was walking along the hallway towards her. He was wearing jeans and the tee shirt she

liked and—he was smiling. 'I've been looking for you!'

She felt her heart exploding softly in her
chest. She shifted on her feet, tried to breathe
calmly. 'I was looking for you too…obvi-
ously…since I'm standing outside your door.'
She gave a little shrug, held the box out towards him. 'I've got this. It's for you…and
Alessia.'

His eyes were so full of light and warmth
that it was hard to hold his gaze. 'A present?
I'm excited—can I open it now?'

She couldn't help smiling. 'Of course.' She
stepped aside so he could unlock the door then
she followed him inside.

Alessia's doll's house was spread open on
the sitting room floor, a clutter of miniature
chairs and beds and dolls strewn around. Still
no pictures on the walls. His guitar wasn't on
its stand.

'Mind your feet. Tiny dolls are the choice
weapon of any self-respecting three-year-old!'
He flashed her a smile, put the box down onto
the sofa. 'Now, what have we got here?' He
seemed ridiculously happy. Surely it couldn't
be just her present… Maybe he'd pulled off
some big business deal.

She watched him lifting the lid, heard him
catch his breath, watched his eyes flit along

the row of pictures, and then he was turning to her, the look in his eyes making her dizzy.

'It's beautiful.' His voice sounded hoarse. He cleared his throat. 'I never expected...' He lifted the frame out of the box, held it at arm's length, looking at the pictures, smiling, just smiling.

She struggled to find her own voice. 'I'm glad you like it. I hope Alessia likes it too.'

'She'll love it, I know she will.' He put it down on the sofa. 'Thank you, Liv. It's such a lovely gift. We don't have many pictures taken together.' He looked around the room. 'You'll have to tell me where to hang it. I'm useless at things like that—it's why the walls are bare.'

She didn't need him to say the rest, that Isabella would have known where to hang their pictures, which light fittings would have looked best on the walls.

He ran a hand through his hair and stepped towards her. 'I was looking for you because I wanted to say sorry about the other day...'

'You don't have to be sorry.' She shrugged. 'We had to talk it out...' She felt his hands closing around hers, warm and tight. It wasn't what she was expecting.

'Sometimes words mess things up, don't you think?'

There was a mischievous glint in his eyes,

something that was making her feel tingly inside. 'I suppose, but sometimes—' She felt his finger on her lips, a little warm pressure. She stopped talking, fought the urge to kiss his finger. He was looking at her and she could see a secret burning in his eyes, a little smile lifting the corners of his mouth.

'I want to show you something and, until I've shown you, will you promise not to say a word?'

The way he was looking at her was turning her inside out. She couldn't have said a word even if she'd wanted to. She nodded.

He smiled. 'Okay then... Let's go.'

As he drove she found it hard not to stare at him. She could feel the energy thrumming through him, see it in the way he was holding himself and in the way he moved. Shifting through the gears, steering around the bends. He was on fire and she was beside herself with curiosity, tingling from head to toe.

In Ravello he parked the car and took her hand. He led her through the narrow alley where she'd seen the lemons, past the tourist shops with their racks of postcards and shelves bursting with limoncello bottles. He sidestepped tourists, not hurrying, not dawdling but pulling her onwards. In the *piazza*

someone stopped them to ask for directions
and she caught herself chewing her bottom lip
with frustration.

'Good luck. I hope you find it,' Zach was
saying and then he looked at her, a twinkle in
his eyes. 'Sorry about that...' His hand closed
around hers again and he pulled her on across
the *piazza*, then turned left, striding up a familiar road. Where the road forked, he led her
onto the narrow walkway, the one next to the
gardens where they'd had their talk and then
a little distance beyond that he stopped. He
was smiling at her, a little glint in his eye. She
looked around, not sure what she was supposed
to be looking for, and then she noticed a pair
of heavy doors with a canopy above, folded
back. She stepped closer. It looked like Marcello's bar, all closed up. She turned to face
him, felt a frown creasing her forehead. Why
had he brought her here?

He held her gaze, then slowly he pulled a
key from his pocket and stepped towards the
door. For some reason she was starting to cry
and then she was laughing, and she wanted to
say something but the words wouldn't come
out, so she let him lead her inside and, inside,
she could hardly believe her eyes. Thousands
of tea lights were flickering on the tables in
the dark recesses of the bar, and in the centre

of the room, under the dome, there was a single chair, a microphone stand and his guitar.

He seated her at a table, touched her face gently. 'Don't say a word, remember,' and then he was settling himself onto the chair, lifting the guitar onto his lap. He plucked the strings softly, strummed a chord, then lifted his eyes to hers.

'Olivia Gardner, in this bar, which I now own jointly with Marcello Moretti, I am literally going to play my heart out for you.'

As his fingers moved over the strings, as she heard the first notes of Fauré's *Pavane*, she felt goosebumps rising on her arms and a hot thick mess of tears behind her eyes and she could hardly breathe because the music was so beautiful, and because her heart was so full of love for him.

As he played he was picturing her face the first time he'd seen it. She'd been looking down at him from the balcony at Kensall Manor. He could see in his mind the way her cheeks had lifted into a smile, that little blush, the way her eyes had glowed. Trapped in her gaze he'd felt at home, would have happily stayed there in the hall, just looking at her, and then he remembered her face as she got off the bus in Ravello, excited eyes, wide smile…running her hand over the wing of his car, mischievous...and their water fight, that demon glint in her eye as she'd stepped towards him with the brimming plastic teapot, Alessia's throaty laughter echoing off the walls. The way she'd looked on the boat, hair blowing, her eyes laying him bare...their first kiss.

He put it all into the music, felt as if he was playing his own heartstrings, and he wanted her to feel it in the depth of her soul because the music could say it so much better than his words ever could. When he played the final note and lifted his eyes, her hands were pressed to her face, which was wet with tears. Perhaps she'd heard every word he'd been playing. He put the guitar down and stood up.

She was getting to her feet, wiping her eyes with her hands, smiling through a fresh wave of tears. 'I don't know what to say, Zach. That was so beautiful—all of this is beautiful.' She stepped closer, looked around then turned back to him. 'You actually *bought* the bar?'

'Half of it, strictly speaking—Marcello's brother's share.'

'When?'

He smiled. 'The day before yesterday.' She started to speak, seemed to be struggling to find words so he carried on. 'It took me a while to work everything out—but what you said to me in the gardens, about running a wedding empire… Well, you were right! It doesn't excite me—'

'But… Lucia said you've bought another wedding venue!'

'We are—in the process of, anyway, but if the sale goes through there's a manager in place. My involvement will be minimal.' He took a step towards her. 'I was on my way back from the viewing when I started thinking about music and all the things you said—and all the things I said—and I started to see that maybe there was a way to have it all.' He closed the distance between them and took her hands in his. 'You reminded me how alive I feel when I'm playing. It's a feeling I don't get from running the business, but I'm never going to play Carnegie Hall and I wouldn't want to anyway. I like my life here.'

He felt a smile tugging at his lips. 'But Ravello *is* the city of music—and, as I was driving home, I remembered Marcello saying he might have to give this place up—and suddenly I had this crazy idea. So I stopped in to have a chat with him and, before I knew it, we were planning a guest list of musicians, talking about adding a mezzanine floor. With such extensive plans in place, it seemed only proper to make him an offer for his brother's half.'

'Zach, please tell me that you haven't done all this for me.'

Her serious tone threw him for a moment and then he saw in her eyes what she was saying. He lifted a hand to her face, traced his thumb over her cheekbone. 'No, I did it for myself because music is what I love, and I did it for you because you asked me to be true to myself.'

She leaned in to his hand, smiled softly. 'That's the right answer.'

He gazed at her, saw the love light in her eyes mingling with the flickering flames of a thousand tea lights, and he knew that this was the right moment. 'Liv, I know we haven't known each other that long, but from the first moment I saw you I felt a connection.' He smiled. 'I know things haven't been easy but I think we've got potential, don't you?'

'Potential?'

'I want you to stay… I want you to help me hang my pictures, I want you to teach Alessia more silly songs, and I want to play my guitar for you every night.' A tear was rolling down her cheek. He followed it with his thumb, gently pushed it away. 'I love you. I want you to marry me… Will you marry me, Olivia?'

Her eyes were glistening now…and she was pressing her lips together, and then a lit-

tle smile broke through and she was laughing
and crying… 'Yes, yes, I will.'

He felt a wave of relief followed by a wave of
euphoria. He pulled her into his arms, swung
her around and laughed. 'You've really got to
stop crying now because I want to kiss you.'

CHAPTER ELEVEN

Eight months later...

'STEP AWAY FROM the window, darling—the light's too harsh.'

'I told you it would be—it always works best over there, near the wardrobe.'

Ralph lowered his camera and mock-scowled. 'And so the pupil becomes the master!'

'You were a good teacher.' She spun round, took up position in front of the large mahogany wardrobe and struck a pose. 'Thanks for stepping up, Ralph. I'm no good on this side of the camera and if I have to go through it I'd rather go through it with you than anyone else.' She looked down at the bouquet in her hands then looked up and smiled.

'Keep it! Don't move, darling—you look amazing.'

She laughed. 'I know for a fact you say that to all your brides.'

'Ah! But today I mean it. You *do* look amazing—but you need to stop talking so we can get the job done.'

She smiled, turned this way and that, lifted her chin, dropped her shoulder, perched on the bed, looked lovingly into the lens, laughed over and over again, mostly for real because it felt weird.

He put the camera down, glanced at his watch and wiped his forehead on his shirt sleeve. 'Where's your father?'

'He's on his way.' She put a hand on his arm. 'Ralph, I want you to relax. It's a very informal wedding—just take happy pictures, okay. They don't need to be perfect.'

A knock on the door made her jump.

Ralph lifted an eyebrow. 'It looks like you need to take your own advice!'

She couldn't deny that she was jittery. If she wasn't such a bag of nerves she'd have been laughing at herself. All those years dreaming of this day, and now all she wanted was to skip to the part where Zach was beside her, holding her hand. She crossed the room and opened the door.

'Dad!'

He seemed to sway a bit at the sight of her and then she could see a tell-tale glisten at the edge of his eyes, could feel her own welling up.

'Oh, Liv...' His mouth was wobbling. 'You look—'

She swallowed hard, flowed into his arms. 'Dad, will you stop it—you're setting me off.' He was holding her in his big bear hug and even the new fabric smell of his wedding day suit couldn't mask the comforting scent of him that she remembered from childhood, from all the times he'd held her like this before. She closed her eyes, let the moment linger...

After the dust had settled from Zach's proposal and after she'd completed her last wedding shoot, she'd gone back to England to tell her mum and dad she was getting married. She'd spent time with her mum in Sussex, then stayed for a week with her dad in North Wales.

Mending their fences had been easier than she imagined. They'd talked about the past, but mostly they'd got on with living in the present. He'd taken her swimming in another freezing sea, and afterwards there'd been hot chocolate out of a dented old flask. He'd marched her to the top of Mount Snowdon and back down again. In the pub he'd got steamed up about plastic pollution and global warming, talked about petitions and about what was going on in the Green Party and she'd listened, felt his passion and fury, potent as ever.

Suddenly she became aware of Ralph clicking away and she stepped out of her dad's arms, but he kept a hold of her shoulders, looked at her with a little glimmer of inkling in his eyes. 'You're glowing, Liv,' and then he beamed, dropped his hands and rifled in his pockets for a handkerchief.

She felt a little colour rising in her cheeks, glanced at Ralph, but he was busy positioning her bouquet on a table near the window so he could take a picture of it. 'It's my wedding day, Dad—of course I'm glowing. I'm happy!' She smoothed the front of her dress, cleared her throat. 'Now, are you absolutely sure about walking me up the aisle? I know it's not really your bag.'

'It's what you want that counts.' He mopped his eyes and smiled. 'It's your day, and I'm here for you… I'll always be here for you.'

She could feel a lump thickening in her throat, laughed as she snatched a tissue from a box on the table. 'You're going to have to stop saying things like that or I'll have to get the make-up artist to come back.'

The door rattled, opened jerkily and Alessia's face appeared in the gap. Her little mouth stiffened for a moment, eyes widened, and then she ran over, wrapped her arms around Olivia's legs.

'You look *so* pretty!'

'And so do you! Very pretty. Has Daddy seen you in your dress yet?'

Alessia shook her head, spoke in a theatrical whisper. 'No! Nonna said it had to be a surprise.'

Olivia laughed, bent down to kiss her. As she felt Alessia's arms sliding around her neck she thought about Izzy, how she had never felt her own daughter's embrace, and she closed her eyes to let the sadness wash over her and subside. It was strange, she thought, how much she'd opened her heart and mind to Izzy after Zach had made his grand gesture, after he'd asked her to marry him. The house had settled into being a home, no more east and west.

Absently, she started pulling out the skirt of Alessia's dress, the pale lemon silk rustling in her fingers. She'd found little soft shoes to match and Alessia had declared that they were *dancing shoes*. Now Alessia was busy pointing her toes, sketching out a little dance on the spot as Olivia fanned out the skirt and pulled the petticoats straight. The hairstylist had woven the same little yellow flowers and Gypsophila into Alessia's hair that she was wearing in her own and the final result was perfect. Zach was going to be even more smitten with his daughter than he already was.

Zach! The love of her life. Just the thought of him was enough to make her heart leap with joy. She pictured his face, the way the little lines around his eyes crinkled when he smiled, the blue of his irises sparkling like sunlight and starlight mixed together.

He and Marcello had done so well with the bar. They'd commissioned Milo to design and put in a mezzanine, and they'd added a few other refinements: a new canopy for the entrance, adjustable lighting. They'd rebranded the place, called it Pavane, which had made her smile. She'd taken the photographs, built a website, while they focused on forward-booking a succession of guest musicians. The official launch had been a nerve-racking success and Zach had been walking on air ever since…

Suddenly she realised that Alessia had stopped dancing and was staring at her. She smiled, checked the sash at the back of Alessia's dress and stood up.

Ralph had her bouquet in his hands, passed it to her. 'Right, you two, let's grab some pictures and then it'll be show time.'

* * *

'Today, Olivia, I join my life to yours, not only as your husband but as your friend, your lover and your confidant...' His voice was clear, self-assured. She could feel the warmth of his hands around hers, the warmth of the spring sunshine on her back, and in his eyes she could see so many things—love, trust, honesty. Desire. 'I want to be the shoulder you lean on, the rock on which you rest, the companion of your life.' She watched his lips moving, felt his words settling into her heart. He paused, smiled softly. 'From this day forward I will walk beside you. My path is now your path. I am yours, for ever.'

The celebrant was turning to her now, giving her a little nod. She felt a smile tugging at her lips, a little lump in her throat as she fastened her eyes on his.

'Zach...what can I say that I haven't already said? What can I give to you that I haven't already given? My body, my mind, my soul and my heart. They're all yours.' His eyes were glistening. She felt a tear sliding down her cheek. 'Everything that I have. Everything that I am belongs to you from this day forward.' She had to stop again. The depth of emotion she could see in his eyes was almost too much to bear. She felt his hands squeezing hers and she took a big breath. 'And I promise that I shall be yours for ever. I will follow you anywhere you go, everywhere you lead me to. Hand in hand. Heart in heart.'

For a moment she lost herself in his eyes and then the celebrant was asking for the rings and Zach was gazing at her, sliding a ring onto her finger, and then she was pushing a ring onto his and there was a blessing, and she could smell the scent of fresh cut grass and the fragrance of the flowering wisteria but all she could see was him…and then he was taking her face in his hands and she felt his mouth on hers, warm and perfect, and he didn't pull away but kissed her slowly, a long kiss that made the ground sway beneath her feet, and she could hear the guests clapping and laughing, a random 'whoop' and then he broke away, still gazing at her. She saw his lips moving silently, 'I love you,' felt her heart caving in her chest, her cheeks aching with a smile.

And then suddenly Alessia skipped forward and looked up. 'Papà. That was yucky!'

Zach walked to the edge of the terrace and leaned on the parapet. He needed a moment to take it all in, to acclimatise to his happiness. Somehow he was here again on his wedding day, surrounded by family and friends.

He looked down at his left hand, rotated the new platinum ring on his finger. Married! He'd thought it would never happen again. He felt a little smile growing on his lips and looked up. Olivia was mingling with their guests, her eyes glowing, cheeks dimpled in endless smiles. He watched her, bathed in the surge of love and admiration he felt for her.

She was talking to Milo. She had her hand on Milo's arm and their faces were animated, and then Milo was pulling her into an embrace, kissing her cheek, and she was laughing, kissing him back. He remembered how mad with jealousy he'd been when he'd thought… That seemed such a long time ago. He shifted his gaze to the man at Milo's side. His name was Luca, a musician Milo had met at Pavane. The bar seemed to bring people together somehow…

Going into business with Marcello had been a good decision. He was playing more regularly now—playing with other musicians too—living just enough of the old dream to feel energised. And the bar was getting great reviews on the Web, becoming known for its eclectic mix of acts, for being a platform for up-and-coming musicians. It felt great, giving new people a chance to be heard. Ravello—the city of music—the perfect place for a music venue. He was so grateful to Olivia for giving him a nudge in the right direction.

Lucia was walking towards his parents, her new friend Massimo at her side. Zach looked down at his feet to hide his amusement. Liv had guessed ages ago that Lucia had a suitor but she'd kept it to herself, dropped mischievous hints now and again. He'd been the last to know.

He looked up again. Lucia was talking to his mother. His father was sitting in a chair bouncing Alessia on his knee. She was showing him her dancing shoes, talking nineteen to the dozen he could tell. He liked seeing them together, could already see how Alessia could wrap her grandfather around her little finger. It made him chuckle. He'd never learned that art, but at least his father was delighted with Villa Fiori, pleased with the manager, Lorenzo. The bookings were promising for the coming year and the next year would be even better. Casa Isabella was already booked to capacity—that was why he and Olivia had set a date at the end of March—it had been the only free Saturday in spring.

He'd half-expected her to choose somewhere else to get married but, if anything, she seemed fonder of the house now than she'd ever been. It was as if she'd bonded with Izzy somehow—

and she'd melted his heart when she'd said that Izzy was family, that if they married somewhere else then it would be like shutting Izzy out.

They'd had their ceremony in the garden, not on the terrace. Olivia was especially fond of the shady little garden rooms, the arched folly with its rampant clambering wisteria, and they were a small gathering of immediate family and friends so the space had felt intimate. Perfect.

'Are you okay, Zach?'

He turned and smiled. Lucia had joined him, elegant in her red dress. 'Yes. I'm happy— what about you? Are you okay?'

She linked her arm through his. 'Yes. I'm fine. A little sad, but I'm very, very happy for you and Olivia. She's…she's good for you, Zach, and Alessia loves her so much.'

He felt a lump rising in his throat and nodded.

Lucia drew in a breath, looked over the terrace then lifted her eyes to the house. 'I think Isabella is at peace now, knowing that you are loved and that Alessia has a mamma. I feel her, you know…and I think she's happy today.'

Zach looked down, saw that Lucia's eyes were wet. He put his arm around her shoulders, pulled her against him. 'I couldn't have managed without you, you know that, don't you? You've been a tower of strength for me and for Alessia and I want to thank you from the bottom of my heart.'

She sniffed, sighed a little. 'You helped me too, Zach. Letting me stay here, letting me look after Alessia—it helped. Being useful took my mind off things a little bit...'

He shifted his gaze back to the terrace, watched Olivia talking to her mum and dad. Family. It was so important. He was glad she'd made up with her dad. He could see how close they were, could see it in their eyes and in their body language as they chatted.

Olivia turned her face, caught his eye, lit up as if she had a little beacon inside. The way she looked in her ivory silk dress, the simple neckline sitting just below her collarbone, the soft fabric flowing around her legs as she moved. He wanted to take her into a quiet part of the garden, pull her close, kiss her slowly, deeply, feel her body pressed against his. The thought of it was making him dizzy.

'You should go to her, Zach. I can tell you want to...and the way she's looking at you— she wants you too.' Lucia patted his arm. 'Go...go!'

He kissed Lucia's cheek then walked to

Olivia's side. He slipped his arm around her waist, leaned in to her ear. 'I'd like to spend some time alone with my wife.'

Her breath warmed his cheek. 'You must have been reading my mind.'

'Let's go!' He lifted two glasses of champagne from a passing tray, handed her one and led her into the garden, through the shady rooms she loved. At the folly where they'd exchanged their vows he stopped, turned to face her.

She had the strangest look in her eye, a warm, glowing, secret look which was turning him inside out. He reached for her hand. 'Have you any idea how lovely you look? How happy you've made me today?'

She smiled. 'So you couldn't be happier...?'

'No! I absolutely couldn't.' He lifted his glass, touched it to hers. 'Here's to you, my beautiful, amazing wife.' He put the glass to his lips, felt the cool champagne tingling on his tongue, then realised suddenly that she hadn't moved. She was looking at him, glass in hand. He felt a frown creasing his forehead. 'What's wrong, Liv?'

She looked down at her feet, seemed to be smiling, and then she looked up. 'I can't drink this.'

'Why—?' The word escaped from his lips

a nanosecond before the penny dropped and then he was staring at her, looking into her eyes, just to make sure he'd got it right. He swallowed, found his voice. 'You're—? No! We're—?'

She was smiling and nodding, her eyes sparkling. 'Yes!'

He felt the glass slipping from his fingers, heard it land on the grass. 'When did you—? How…?'

'A couple of days ago—I've been so busy with the wedding that I hadn't noticed I was late.' He watched as she put her glass down on the folly step. 'I'm only six weeks. As to how—' She pulled a thinking face. 'I think you know!'

'So you couldn't be happier?'

Just moments ago she'd asked him that, and now he thought he might actually burst. Slowly, he reached his hands to her waist, looked at the way her dress fell straight down over her flat stomach. He dropped to his knees, kissed the place where the new life was growing, whispered, 'Hello, baby.'

And then he felt Olivia's fingers in his hair and he remembered why he'd wanted to be alone with her.

He stood up, cupped her face tenderly in his hands and kissed her slowly, deeply. He felt her body rising to his and then he was losing himself in the warm smell of her skin, the scent of her perfume and the fragrance of wisteria drifting on the gentle breeze.

* * * * *

If you enjoyed this story,
check out this other great read from
Ella Hayes

Her Brooding Scottish Heir

Available now!